Joel Chandler Harris

ON THE PLANTATION

A STORY OF A GEORGIA BOY'S ADVENTURES DURING THE WAR

JOEL CHANDLER HARRIS

Illustrated by E. W. Kemble

Foreword by Erskine Caldwell

BROWN THRASHER BOOKS
THE UNIVERSITY OF GEORGIA PRESS
ATHENS

Foreword by Erskine Caldwell copyright © 1980 by the
University of Georgia Press, Athens, Georgia 30602

Library of Congress Catalog Card Number 79-5189
International Standard Book Number
0-8203-0494-8
0-8203-0495-6 pbk.

On the Plantation was first published in 1892
by D. Appleton and Company, New York.

CONTENTS

FOREWORD

Joel Chandler Harris was one of Georgia's talented writers and a worthy American author.

The enduring fame of Joel Harris as a skillful storyteller had its beginning with the publication of the first of his enchanting *Uncle Remus* stories. These and other local-color tales were written to sound as if they were being told to a group of small children on a winter night beside the blazing fireplace of a middle Georgia farmhouse. And ever since his stories first appeared in print, it has yet to be resolved who enjoys them the most—a child or the adult reading them aloud.

The recognition by readers and critics of Joel Harris as a writer of captivating fiction occurred when he was still a young man in his thirties. Thereafter his reputation as a teller of tales was constantly enhanced over the years with the creation of *Br'er Rabbit* and numerous other animal fables.

On the Plantation, one of Harris's many books depicting Georgia scenes, was partly factual and partly fictional—a rarely accomplished literary feat—although essentially it is an autobiographical novel. It was written during the middle period of his constantly active career, which came to an untimely end at the age of sixty.

The reading of the Harris fables in early times was not confined to Georgians alone, or even to Southerners; his works were read and enjoyed nationwide long before the end of the past century. And at the beginning of the present century, Joel Chandler Harris was honored in New York by his peers who elected him to membership in the exclusive American Academy of Arts and Letters. The induction ceremony took place in 1905. On the same occasion, together with Harris, some of the American authors likewise honored were Thomas Bailey Aldrich, Henry James, Charles Eliot Norton, Mark Twain, Theodore Roosevelt, and Henry Adams.

The simplicity of his style of writing, the telling description of scenes, the unadorned wording of his sentences provide evidence of Joel

Harris's storytelling genius, and this is readily found from the very beginning of *On the Plantation*. However, as the novel progresses, the first-time reader of Joel Harris is likely to become perplexed and even mildly bewildered by the literal transcription of unfamiliar Georgia plantation Negro-Geechee speech. Although the reader may have mastered the nuances of traditional Deep South accents and inflections, he still will find himself relying upon Harris's rendition for what otherwise might be mistaken for a foreign language. As it is, Harris slowly and artfully introduces the reader to the authentic Geechee dialect—one of the dialects which for more than a century the white Southerner has unwittingly emulated while cultivating his richly intoned accent.

The Geechee sounds are so rhythmical and spellbinding that, even when voiced by a white person or animal characters, the black person's speech becomes such perfected dialect that any attempt to render Geechee into anything more than tolerable English would result in pages of incomprehensible gibberish. But to whatever extent the reader may be temporarily baffled by the unfamiliar speech, it is not unlikely that he will soon become so intrigued by the magical sounds that he will find himself doing his reading aloud for his own amusement as he eagerly turns pages.

In the hands of Joel Harris, the transcription of Geechee dialect has resulted in clear and concise and always readable prose. In South Carolina another southern writer, Ambrose Gonzales, devoted much of his life to transcribing with utmost fidelity the stories told to him by African slaves and their descendants in Charleston and the Carolina low country in their Gullah dialect. Whatever may be the merits of the methods used by Harris and Gonzales, the results differ. While the Gullah of Ambrose Gonzales is authentic to the extreme, its genuineness often makes it obscure in meaning if not downright unintelligible to the unprepared reader. The Geechee of Harris, while its authenticity is no less evident, is tempered and relieved by the artistry of the author.

The subtitle of *On the Plantation*—"A Story of a Georgia Boy's Adventures during the War"—avoided the possibility of arousing sensitive feelings in the North and the South when the book was published in the aftermath of "the War." Confederate money is freely mentioned,

wounded soldiers return to Georgia from battle-
fields in Virginia, and Yankee soldiers are
friendly when not being hostile. Since the
Spanish-American War and both world wars
were far in the future, and the Revolutionary
War was far in the past, the reference to "the
War" was a thoughtful and tactful way of assuag-
ing the emotional and psychic wounds that had
been inflicted upon all Americans by four years
of bitter warfare otherwise known as the Civil
War and the War between the States.

All wars aside, this interesting and eloquent
story depicting a small but significant segment of
American life in earlier years has succeeded in
surviving the ravages of time. Consequently it
has earned the right to be included in the library
of memorable southern novels.

ERSKINE CALDWELL
Scottsdale, Arizona

INTRODUCTORY NOTE.

SOME of my friends who have read in serial form the chronicles that follow profess to find in them something more than an autobiographical touch. Be it so. It would indeed be difficult to invest the commonplace character and adventures of Joe Maxwell with the vitality that belongs to fiction. Nevertheless, the lad himself, and the events which are herein described, seem to have been born of a dream. That which is fiction pure and simple in these pages bears to me the stamp of truth, and that which is true reads like a clumsy invention. In this matter it is not for me to prompt the reader. He must sift the fact from the fiction and label it to suit himself.

J. C. H.

TO THE MEMORY OF

JOSEPH ADDISON TURNER

LAWYER, EDITOR, SCHOLAR, PLANTER, AND PHILANTHROPIST

THIS MIXTURE OF FACT AND FICTION

IS INSCRIBED

ON THE PLANTATION.

CHAPTER I.

JOE MAXWELL MAKES A START.

THE post-office in the middle Georgia vil-
lage of Hillsborough used to be a queer little
place, whatever it is now. It was fitted up in
a cellar; and the postmaster, who was an enterprising gentleman from Connecticut, had arranged matters so that those who went after
their letters and papers could at the same time
get their grocery supplies.

Over against the wall on one side was a
faded green sofa. It was not an inviting seat,
for in some places the springs peeped through,
and one of its legs was broken, giving it a suspicious tilt against the wall. But a certain little boy found one corner of the rickety old
sofa a very comfortable place, and he used to

curl up there nearly every day, reading such stray newspapers as he could lay hands on, and watching the people come and go.

To the little boy the stock of goods displayed for sale was as curious in its variety as the people who called day after day for the letters that came or that failed to come. To some dainty persons the mingled odor of cheese, camphene, and mackerel would have been disagreeable; but Joe Maxwell—that was the name of the little boy—had a healthy disposition and a strong stomach, and he thought the queer little post-office was one of the pleasantest places in the world.

A partition of woodwork and wire netting cut off the post-office and the little stock of groceries from the public at large, but outside of that was an area where a good many people could stand and wait for their letters. In one corner of this area was the rickety green sofa, and round about were chairs and boxes and barrels on which tired people could rest themselves.

The Milledgeville papers had a large circulation in the county. They were printed at the capital of the State, and were thought to be very important on that account. They had so many readers in the neighborhood that the postmaster, in order to save time and trouble, used to pile them up on a long shelf outside the wooden partition, where each subscriber could help himself. Joe Maxwell took advantage of this method, and on Tuesdays, when the Milledgeville papers arrived, he could always be found curled up in the corner of the old green sofa reading the *Recorder* and the *Federal Union*. What he found in those papers to interest him it would be hard to say. They were full of political essays that were popular in those days, and they had long reports of political conventions and meetings from all parts of the State. They were papers for grown people, and Joe Maxwell was only twelve years old, and small for his age.

There was another place that Joe found it pleasant to visit, and that was a lawyer's office in one of the rooms of the old tavern that looked out on the pillared veranda. It was a pleasant place to him, not because it was a law-office, but because it was the office of a gentleman who was very friendly to the youngster. The gentleman's name was Mr. Deometari, and

Joe called him Mr. Deo, as did the other people of Hillsborough. He was fat and short and wore whiskers, which gave him a peculiar appearance at that time. All the rest of the men that Joe knew wore either a full beard or a mustache and an imperial. For that reason Mr. Deometari's whiskers were very queer-looking. He was a Greek, and there was a rumor among the people about town that he had been compelled to leave his country on account of his politics. Joe never knew until long afterward that politics could be a crime. He thought that politics consisted partly in newspaper articles signed " Old Subscriber" and " Many Citizens " and " Vox Populi" and " Scrutator," and partly in arguments between the men who sat in fine weather on the dry-goods boxes under the china-trees. But there was a mystery about Mr. Deometari, and it pleased the lad to imagine all sorts of romantic stories about the fat lawyer. Although Mr. Deometari was a Greek, there was no foreign twang to his tongue. Only as close an observer as the boy could have told from his talk that he was a foreigner. He was a good lawyer and a good speaker, and all the other lawyers seemed to like him. They

enjoyed his company so well that it was only
occasionally that Joe found him in his office
alone.   Once Mr. Deometari took from his

Mr. Deometari put on his uniform.

closet a military uniform and put it on.   Joe
Maxwell thought it was the most beautiful uniform he had ever seen.   Gold braid ran down

the sides of the trousers, gold cords hung loosely on the breast of the coat, and a pair of tremendous epaulets surmounted the shoulders. The hat was something like the hats Joe had seen in picture-books. It was caught up at the sides with little gold buttons, and trimmed with a long black feather that shone like a pigeon's breast. Fat as Mr. Deometari was, the lad thought he looked very handsome in his fine uniform. This was only one incident. In his room, which was a large one, Mr. Deometari had boxes packed with books, and he gave Joe leave to ransack them. Many of the volumes were in strange tongues, but among them were some quaint old English books, and these the lad relished beyond measure. After a while Mr. Deometari closed his office and went away to the war.

It would not be fair to say that Joe was a studious lad. On the contrary, he was of an adventurous turn of mind, and he was not at all fond of the books that were in his desk at Hillsborough Academy. He was full of all sorts of pranks and capers, and there were plenty of people in the little town ready to declare that he would come to some bad end if he was not more frequently dosed with what the old folks used to call hickory oil.   Some of Joe Maxwell's pranks were commonplace, but others were ingenious enough to give him quite a reputation for humor, and one prank in particular is talked of by the middle-aged people of Hillsborough to this day.

The teacher of the academy had organized a military company among the pupils—it was just about the time when rumors and hints of war had begun to take shape—and a good deal of interest was felt in the organization, especially by the older boys.   Of this company Joe Maxwell was the fourth corporal, a position which gave him a place at the foot of the company. The Hillsborough Cadets drilled every schoolday, and sometimes on Saturdays, and they soon grew to be very proud of their proficiency.

At last, after a good deal of manœuvring on the playgrounds and in the public square, the teacher, who was the captain, concluded that the boys had earned a vacation, and it was decided that the company should go into camp for a week on the Oconee River, and fish and hunt and have a good time generally.   The boys fairly went wild when the announcement was made, and some of them wanted to hug the teacher, who had hard work to explain that an attempt of this sort was not in accord with military tactics or discipline.

All the arrangements were duly made. Tents were borrowed from the Hillsborough Rifles, and the drum corps of that company was hired to make music. A half-dozen wagons carried the camp outfit and the small boys, while the larger ones marched. It was an entirely new experience for Joe Maxwell, and he enjoyed it as only a healthy and high-spirited boy could enjoy it. The formal and solemn way in which the guard was mounted was very funny to him, and the temptation to make a joke of it was too strong to be resisted.

The tents were pitched facing each other, with the officers' tent at the head of the line thus formed. At the other end of the lane and a little to the rear was the baggage-tent, in which the trunks, boxes, and commissaries were stored. Outside of all, the four sentinels marched up and down. The tents were pitched in an old field that was used as a pasture, and Joe noticed during the afternoon two mules and a horse

browsing around. He noticed, too, that these
animals were very much disturbed, especially
when the drums began to beat, and that their
curiosity would not permit them to get very far
from the camp, no matter how frightened they
were.

It happened that one of Joe's messmates was
to go on guard duty at twelve o'clock that
night. He was a fat, awkward, good-natured
fellow, this messmate, and a heavy sleeper, too,
so that, when the corporal of the guard under-
took to arouse him, all the boys in the tent were
awakened. All except Joe quickly went to sleep
again, but this enterprising youngster quietly
put on his clothes, and, in the confusion of
changing the guard, slipped out of the lines
and hid in a convenient gully not far from the
camp.

It was his intention to worry if not to fright-
en his messmate, and while he lay there trying
to think out the best plan to pursue, he heard
the horse and mules trampling and snorting not
very far off. Their curiosity was not yet satisfied, and they seemed to be making their way
toward the camp for the purpose of reconnoi-
tering. Joe's mind was made up in an instant.

He slipped down the gully until the animals were between him and the camp, and then, seizing a large pine brush that happened to be lying near, he sprang toward them. The mules and horse were ripe for a stampede. The camp itself was an object of suspicion, and this attack from an unexpected quarter was too much for them. Snorting with terror they rushed in the direction of the tents. The sleepy sentinel, hearing them coming, fired his gun in the air and ran yelling into the camp, followed by the horse and one of the mules. The other mule shied to the right when the gun was fired, and ran into the baggage-tent. There was a tremendous rattle and clatter of boxes, pots, pans, and crockery ware. The mule, crazed with fright, made a violent effort to get through the tent, but it caught him in some way. Finally, the ropes that held it down gave way, and the mule, with the tent flapping and flopping on his back, turned and rushed through the camp. To all but Joe Maxwell it was a horrifying sight. Many of the boys, as the saying is, "took to the woods," and some of them were prostrated with fright. These were consequences that Joe had not counted on, and it was a long time before he confessed

to his share in the night's sport. The results
reached further than the camp. In another part
of the plantation the negroes were holding a revival meeting in the open air, preaching and
shouting and singing. Toward this familiar
scene the mule made his way, squealing, bray-
ing, and kicking, the big white tent flopping on
his back. As the terrified animal circled around
the place, the negroes cried out that Satan had
come, and the panic that ensued among them
is not easily described. Many thought that the
apparition was the ushering in of the judgment-
day, while by far the greater number firmly believed that the " Old Boy " himself was after
them. The uproar they made could be plainly
heard at the camp, more than a mile away—
shrieks, screams, yells, and cries for mercy.
After it was all over, and Joe Maxwell had
crept quietly to bed, the thought came to him
that it was not such a fine joke, after all, and he
lay awake a long time repenting the night's
work. He heard the next day that nobody had
been hurt and that no serious damage had been
done, but it was many weeks before he forgave
himself for his thoughtless prank.

Although Joe was fond of fun, and had a

great desire to be a clown in a circus or to be the driver of a stage-coach—just such a red and yellow coach, with " U. S. M." painted on its doors, as used to carry passengers and the mails between Hillsborough and Rockville—he never permitted his mind to dwell on these things. He knew very well that the time would soon come when he would have to support his mother and himself. This thought used to come to him again and again when he was sitting in the little post-office, reading the Milledgeville papers.

It so happened that these papers grew very interesting to both old and young as the days went by. The rumors of war had developed into war itself. In the course of a few months two companies of volunteers had gone to Virginia from Hillsborough, and the little town seemed to be lonelier and more deserted than ever. Joe Maxwell noticed, as he sat in the post-office, that only a very few old men and ladies came after the letters and papers, and he missed a great many faces that used to smile at him as he sat reading, and some of them he never saw again. He noticed, too, that when there had been a battle or a skirmish the ladies and young girls came to the post-office more frequently. When the news was very important, one of the best-known citizens would mount a chair or a dry-goods box and read the telegrams aloud to the waiting and anxious group of people, and sometimes the hands and the voice of the reader trembled.

One day while Joe Maxwell was sitting in the post-office looking over the Milledgeville papers, his eye fell on an advertisement that interested him greatly. It seemed to bring the whole world nearer to him. The advertisement set forth the fact that on next Tuesday the first number of *The Countryman*, a weekly paper would be published. It would be modeled after Mr. Addison's little paper, the *Spectator*, Mr. Goldsmith's little paper, the *Bee*, and Mr. Johnson's little paper, the *Rambler*. It would be edited by J. A. Turner, and it would be issued on the plantation of the editor, nine miles from Hillsborough. Joe read this advertisement over a dozen times, and it was with a great deal of impatience that he waited for the next Tuesday to come.

But the day did come, and with it came the first issue of *The Countryman*. Joe read it from

beginning to end, advertisements and all, and
he thought it was the most entertaining little
paper he had ever seen. Among the interesting things was an announcement by the editor
that he wanted a boy to learn the printing
business. Joe borrowed pen and ink and some
paper from the friendly postmaster, and wrote
a letter to the editor, saying that he would be
glad to learn the printing business. The letter
was no doubt an awkward one, but it served its
purpose, for when the editor of *The Countryman*
came to Hillsborough he hunted Joe up, and
told him to get ready to go to the plantation.
The lad, not without some misgivings, put away
his tops and marbles, packed his little belong-
ings in an old-fashioned trunk, kissed his mother
and his grandmother good-by, and set forth on
what turned out to be the most important journey of his life.

Sitting in the buggy by the side of the editor and publisher of *The Countryman*, Joe Maxwell felt lonely indeed, and this feeling was in-
creased as he went through the little town and
heard his schoolmates, who were at their marbles on the public square, bidding him good-
by. He could hardly keep back his tears at

this, but, on looking around after the buggy had gone a little way, he saw his friends had returned to their marbles, and the thought struck him that he was already forgotten. Many and many a time after that he thought of his little companions and how quickly they had returned to their marbles.

The editor of *The Countryman* must have divined what was passing in the lad's mind (he was a quick-witted man and a clever one, too), for he tried to engage in conversation with Joe. But the boy preferred to nurse his loneliness, and would only talk when he was compelled to answer a question. Finally, the editor asked him if he would drive, and this Joe was glad enough to do, for there is some diversion in holding the reins over a spirited horse. The editor's horse was a large gray, named Ben Bolt, and he was finer than any of the horses that Joe had seen at the livery-stable. Feeling a new and an unaccustomed touch on the reins, Ben Bolt made an effort to give a new meaning to his name by bolting sure enough. The road was level and hard, and the horse ran rapidly for a little distance; but Joe Maxwell's arms were tough, and before the horse had gone a quarter of a mile the lad had him completely under control.

"You did that very well," said the editor, who was familiar with Ben Bolt's tricks. " I didn't know that little boys in town could drive horses."

"Oh, sometimes they can," replied Joe. "If he had been scared, I think I should have been scared myself; but he was only playing. He has been tied at the rack all day, and he must be hungry."

"Yes," said the editor, "he is hungry, and he wants to see his mate, Rob Roy."

Then the editor, in a fanciful way, went on to talk about Ben Bolt and Rob Roy, as if they were persons instead of horses; but it did not seem fanciful to Joe, who had a strange sympathy with animals of all kinds, especially horses and dogs. It pleased him greatly to think that he had ideas in common with a grown man, who knew how to write for the papers; and if the editor was talking to make Joe forget his loneliness he succeeded admirably, for the lad thought no more of the boys who had so quickly returned to their marbles, but only of his mother, whom he had last seen stand-

ing at the little gate smiling at him through
her tears.

As they drove along the editor pointed out
a little log-cabin near the road.

He talks bigger than anybody.

"That," said he, "is where the high sheriff
of the county lives.   Do you know Colonel John
B. Stith?"

"Yes," Joe replied; "but I thought he lived in a large, fine house. I don't see how he can get in at that door yonder."

"What makes you think he is too big for the door?" asked the editor.

"Why, the way he goes on," said Joe, with the bluntness of youth. "He is always in town talking politics, and he talks bigger than anybody."

"Well," said the editor, laughing, "that is his house. When you get a little older you'll find people who are more disappointing than the high sheriff. Boys are sometimes too big for their breeches, I've heard said, but this is the first time I ever heard that a man could be too big for his house. That is a good one on the colonel."

Ben Bolt trotted along steadily and rapidly, but after a while dusk fell, and then the stars came out. Joe peered ahead, trying to make out the road.

"Just let the horse have his way," said the editor. "He knows the road better than I do"; and it seemed to be so, for, when heavy clouds from the west came up and hid the stars, and only the darkness was visible, Ben Bolt trotted along as steadily as ever.   He splashed through Crooked Creek, walked up the long hill, and then started forward more rapidly than ever.

" It is a level road, now," the editor re-marked, "and Ben Bolt is on the home-stretch."

In a little while he stopped before a large gate.   It was opened in a jiffy by some one who seemed to be waiting.

" Is that you, Harbert? " asked the editor.

" Yes, marster."

" Well, I want you to take Mr. Maxwell here to Mr. Snelson's."

" Yasser," responded the negro.

"Snelson is the foreman of the printing-of-fice," the editor explained to Joe, "and for the present you are to board with him. I hope he will make things pleasant for you.   Good-night."

To the lonely lad it seemed a long journey to Mr. Snelson's   through wide plantation gates, down narrow lanes, along a bit of public road, and then a plunge into the depths of a great wood, where presently a light gleamed through.

" I'll hail 'em," said Harbert, and he sent be-fore him into the darkness a musical halloo, whereupon, as promptly as its echo, came a hearty response from the house, with just the faintest touch of the Irish brogue in the voice.

"Ah, and it's the young man! Jump right down and come in to the warmth of the fire. There's something hot on the hearth, where it's waiting you."

And so Joe Maxwell entered on a new life— a life as different as possible from that which he had left behind in Hillsborough.

CHAPTER II.

A PLANTATION NEWSPAPER.

THE printing-office was a greater revelation to Joe Maxwell than it would be to any of the youngsters who may happen to read this. It was a very small affair; the type was old and worn, and the hand-press—a Washington No. 2—had seen considerable service. But it was all new to Joe, and the fact that he was to become a part of the machinery aroused in his mind the most delightful sensations. He quickly mastered the boxes of the printer's case, and before many days was able to set type swiftly enough to be of considerable help to Mr. Snelson, who was foreman, compositor, and pressman.

The one queer feature about *The Countryman* was the fact that it was the only plantation newspaper that has ever been published, the nearest post-office being nine miles away. It might be supposed that such a newspaper would be a failure ; but *The Countryman* was a success from the start, and at one time it reached a circulation of nearly two thousand copies. The editor was a very original writer, and his editorials in *The Countryman* were quoted in all the papers in the Confederacy, but he was happiest when engaged in a political controversy. Another feature of *The Countryman* was the fact that there was never any lack of copy for the foreman and the apprentice to set. Instead of clipping from his exchanges, the editor sent to the office three books, from which extracts could be selected. These books were *Lacon*, Percy's *Anecdotes*, and Rochefoucauld's *Maxims*. Then there were weekly letters from the army in Virginia and voluntary contributions from many ambitious writers. Some of the war correspondence was very gloomy, for as the months wore on it told of the death of a great many young men whom Joe had known, and the most of them had been very kind to him.

The days in the printing-office would have been very lonely for Joe, but the grove that surrounded it was full of gray squirrels. These had been so long undisturbed that they were comparatively tame. They were in the habit of running about over the roof of the office and playing at hide-and-seek like little children. To the roof, too, the blue-jays would bring their acorns and hammer at the hard shells in the noisiest way, and once a red fox made bold to venture near Joe's window, where he stood listening and sniffing the air until some noise caused him to vanish like a flash. Most interesting of all, a partridge and her mate built their nest within a few feet of the window, and it often happened that Joe neglected his work in watching the birds. They bent the long grass over from each side carefully until they had formed a little tunnel three or four feet long. When this was done, Mrs. Partridge made her way to the end of it and began to scratch and flutter just as a hen does when taking a dust-bath. She was hollowing out her nest. By the time the nest was completed the archway of grass that had hid it was considerably disarranged. Then Mrs. Partridge sat quietly on the little hollow she had made, while Mr. Partridge rebuilt the archway over her until she was completely concealed. He was very careful about this. Frequently he would walk

off a little way and turn and look at the nest.
If his sharp eyes could see anything suspicious,
he would return and weave the grass more
closely together. Finally, he seemed to be satisfied with his work. He shook his wings and
began to preen himself, and then Mrs. Partridge came out and joined him. They con-
sulted together with queer little cluckings, and
finally ran off into the undergrowth as if bent
on a frolic.

The work of Mr. and Mrs. Partridge was so
well done that Joe found it very difficult to discover the nest when he went out of the office.
He knew where it was from his window, but
when he came to look for it out of doors it
seemed to have disappeared, so deftly was it
concealed; and he would have been compelled
to hunt for it very carefully but for the fact that
when Mrs. Partridge found herself disturbed
she rushed from the little grass tunnel and
threw herself at Joe's feet, fluttering around as
if desperately wounded, and uttering strange little cries of distress. Once she actually touched
his feet with her wings, but when he stooped to
pick her up she managed to flutter off just out
of reach of his hand. Joe followed along after

Mrs. Partridge for some little distance, and he discovered that the farther she led him away from her nest the more her condition improved, until finally she ran off into the sedge and disappeared. Joe has never been able to find any one to tell him how Mrs. Partridge knew what kind of antics a badly wounded bird would cut up. He has been told that it is the result of instinct. The scientists say, however, that instinct is the outgrowth of necessity ; but it seems hard to believe that necessity could have given Mrs. Partridge such accurate knowledge of the movements of a wounded bird.

In carrying proofs from the printing-office to the editor, Joe Maxwell made two discoveries that he considered very important. One was that there was a big library of the best books at his command, and the other was that there was a pack of well-trained harriers on the plantation. He loved books and he loved dogs, and if he had been asked to choose between the library and the harriers he would have hesitated a long time. The books were more numerous—there were nearly two thousand of them, while there were only five harriers—but in a good many respects the dogs were the liveliest. Fortunately,

Joe was not called on to make any choice.   He had the dogs to himself in the late afternoon and the books at night, and he made the most of both. More than this, he had the benefit of the culture of the editor of *The Countryman* and of the worldly experience of Mr. Snelson, the printer.

To Joe Maxwell, sadly lacking in knowledge of mankind, Mr. Snelson seemed to be the most

Mr. Snelson as Richard III.

engaging of men.   He was the echo and mouthpiece of a world the youngster had heard of but never seen, and it pleased him to hear the genial printer rehearse his experiences, ranging all the way from Belfast, Ireland, where he was born, to all the nooks and corners of the United States, including the little settlement where the plantation newspaper was published. Mr. Snelson had been a tramp and almost a tragedian, and he was pleased on many occasions to give his little apprentice a taste of his dramatic art. He would stuff a pillow under his coat and give readings from *Richard III*, or wrap his wife's mantilla about him and play *Hamlet*. When tired of the stage he would clear his throat and render some of the old ballads, which he sang very sweetly indeed.

One night, after the little domestic concert was over and Joe was reading a book by the light of the pine-knot fire, a great fuss was heard in the hen-house, which was some distance from the dwelling.

"Run, John," exclaimed Mrs. Snelson; "I just know somebody is stealing my dominicker hen and her chickens. Run!"

"Let the lad go," said Mr. Snelson, amiably. "He's young and nimble, and whoever's there he'll catch 'em.—Run, lad! and if ye need help, lift your voice and I'll be wit' ye directly."

The dwelling occupied by Mr. Snelson was in the middle of a thick wood, and at night, when there was no moon, it was very dark out of doors; but Joe Maxwell was not afraid of the dark. He leaped from the door and had reached the hen-house before the chickens ceased cackling and fluttering. It was too dark to see anything, but Joe, in groping his way around, laid his hand on Somebody.

His sensations would be hard to describe. His heart seemed to jump into his mouth, and he felt a thrill run over him from head to foot. It was not fear, for he did not turn and flee. He placed his hand again on the Somebody and asked:

"Who are you?"

Whatever it was trembled most violently and the reply came in a weak, shaking voice and in the shape of another question:

"Is dis de little marster what come fum town ter work in de paper office?"

"Yes; who are you, and what are you doing here?"

"I'm name Mink, suh, an' I b'longs to Marse Tom Gaither. I bin run'd away an' I got dat hongry dat it look like I bleedz ter ketch me a chicken. I bin mighty nigh famished, suh. I wish you'd please, suh, excusen me dis time."

"Why didn't you break and run when you heard me coming?" asked Joe, who was disposed to take a practical view of the matter.

"You wuz dat light-footed, suh, dat I ain't hear you, an' sides dat, I got my han' kotch in dish yer crack, an' you wuz right on top er me 'fo' I kin work it out."

"Why don't you stay at home?" asked Joe.

"Dey don't treat me right, suh," said the negro, simply. The very tone of his voice was more convincing than any argument could have been.

"Can you get your hand out of the crack?" asked Joe.

"Lord, yes, suh; I'd 'a done got it out fo' now, but when you lipt on me so quick all my senses wuz skeered out'n me."

"Well," said Joe, "get your hand out and stay here till I come back, and I'll fetch you something to eat."

"You ain't foolin' me, is you, little marster?"

"Do I look like I'd fool you?" said Joe, scornfully.

"I can't see you plain, suh," said the negro,

drawing a long breath, "but you don't talk like it."

"Well, get your hand loose and wait."

As Joe turned to go to the house, he saw Mr. Snelson standing in the door.

"It's all right, sir," the youngster said. "None of the chickens are gone."

"A great deal of fuss and no feathers," said Mr. Snelson. "I doubt but it was a mink."

"Yes," said Joe, laughing. "It must have been a Mink, and I'm going to set a bait for him."

"In all this dark?" asked the printer. "Why, I could stand in the door and crush it wit' me teeth."

"Why, yes," replied Joe. "I'll take some biscuit and a piece of corn bread, and scatter them around the hen-house, and if the mink comes back he'll get the bread and leave the chickens alone."

"Capital!" exclaimed Mr. Snelson, slapping Joe on the back. "I says to mother here, says I, 'As sure as you're born to die, old woman, that b'y has got the stuff in 'im that they make men out of.' I said them very words. Now didn't I, mother?"

Joe got three biscuits and a pone of corn-

bread and carried them to Mink. The negro
had freed his hand, and he loomed up in the
darkness as tall as a giant.

"Why, you seem to be as big as a horse,"
said Joe.

"Thanky, little marster, thanky. Yes, suh,
I'm a mighty stout nigger, an' ef marster would

Mink.

des make dat overseer lemme 'lone I'd do some
mighty good work, an' I'd a heap druther do it
dan ter be hidin' out in de swamp dis away like
some wil' varmint. Good-night, little marster."

"Good-night!" said Joe.

"God bless you, little marster!" cried Mink,
as he vanished in the darkness.

That night in Joe Maxwell's dreams the voice of the fugitive came back to him, crying, "God bless you, little marster!"

But it was not in dreams alone that Mink came back to Joe. In more than one way the negro played an important part in the lad's life on the plantation. One evening about dusk, as Joe was going home, taking a "near cut" through the Bermuda pasture, a tall form loomed up before him, outlining itself against the sky.

"Howdy, little marster! 'Tain't nobody but Mink. I des come ter tell you dat ef you want anything out'n de woods des sen' me word by Harbert. I got some pa'tridge-eggs here now. Deyer tied up in a rag, but dat don't hurt um. Ef you'll des spread out yo' hank'cher I'll put um in it."

"Haven't you gone home yet?" asked Joe, as he held out his handkerchief.

"Lord, no, suh!" exclaimed the negro. "De boys say dat de overseer say he waitin' fer Mink wid a club."

There were four dozen of these eggs, and Joe and Mr. Snelson enjoyed them hugely.

From that time forward, in one way and another, Joe Maxwell kept in communication with Mink. The lad was not too young to observe that the negroes on the plantation treated him with more consideration than they showed to other white people with the exception of their master. There was nothing they were not ready to do for him at any time of day or night. The secret of it was explained by Harbert, the man-of-all-work around the "big house."

"Marse Joe," said Harbert one day, "I wuz gwine 'long de road de udder night an' I met a great big nigger man. Dish yer nigger man took an' stop me, he did, an' he 'low, 'Dey's a little white boy on yo' place which I want you fer ter keep yo' two eyes on 'im, an' when he say come, you come, an' when he say go, you go.' I 'low, ''hey, big nigger man! what de matter?' an' he 'spon' back, 'I done tole you, an' I ain't gwine tell you no mo'.' So dar you got it, Marse Joe, an' dat de way it stan's."

And so it happened that, humble as these negroes were, they had it in their power to smooth many a rough place in Joe Maxwell's life. The negro women looked after him with almost motherly care, and pursued him with kindness, while the men were always ready to contribute to his pleasure.

CHAPTER III.

TRACKING A RUNAWAY.

ONE Sunday morning, not long after Joe's adventure with Mink, Harbert came to him with a serious face.

"Marse Joe," he said, "dey er gwine ter ketch Mink dis time."

"How do you know?"

"Kaze, soon dis mornin' whiles I wuz a-feedin' de hogs, I seed one er dem Gaither boys comin' down de road under whip an' spur, an' I ax 'im wharbouts he gwine, an' he say he gwine atter Bill Locke an' his nigger dogs. He 'low dat he know whar Mink bin las' Friday night, an' dey gwine ter put de dogs on his track an' ketch 'im. Dey'll be 'long back dis a way terreckly."

The lad had witnessed many a fox-chase and had hunted rabbits hundreds of times, not only with the plantation harriers but with hounds;

but he had never seen a runaway negro hunted down, and he had a boy's curiosity in the matter, as well as a personal interest in the fate of Mink. So he mounted his horse and waited for Mr. Locke and young Gaither to return. He knew Bill Locke well, having seen him often in Hillsborough. Mr. Locke had been an overseer, but he saved money, bought two or three negroes, and had a little farm of his own. He had a great reputation as a negro-hunter, mainly because the hunting of runaways was a part of his business. His two dogs, Music and Sound, were known all over the country, and they were the terror of the negroes, not because they were fierce or dangerous, but because of their sagacity. Sound was a small brown hound, not larger than a beagle, but he had such powers of scent that the negroes regarded him with superstitious awe. He had what is called a "cold nose," which is a short way of saying that he could follow a scent thirty-six hours old, and yet he was a very shabby-looking dog.

When Locke and young Gaither rode by they were joined by Joe Maxwell, and his company seemed to be very welcome, especially to the Gaither boy, who regarded the affair as a

frolic.   Mr. Locke was a man of very few
words.   His face was dark and sallow and his
eyes sunken.   His neck was long and thin, and
Joe observed that his "Adam's apple" was un-
usually large.   As the negroes said, Mr. Locke
and his dogs "favored" each other.   He was
small and puny, and his dogs were small and
scrawny.

"Do you think you'll catch Mink?" asked
Joe.   Mr Locke looked at the lad almost pityingly, and smiled.

"We'll git the nigger," he replied, "if he's
been seed sence Friday noon.   We'll git him
if he ain't took wings.   All I ast of him is to
stay somewheres on top of the ground, and he's
mine."

"Why did the negro run away?" said Joe
to young Gaither.

"Oh, he can't get along with the overseer.
And I don't blame him much.   I told pap this
morning that if I had to choose between Mink
and Bill Davidson I'd take Mink every time.
But the trouble with pap is he's getting old,
and thinks he can't get along without an overseer, and overseers are mighty hard to get now.
I tell you right now that when I get grown I'm

not going to let any overseer bang my niggers around."

Mr. Locke said nothing, but Joe heartily indorsed young Gaither's sentiments.

When they arrived at the Gaither place, Mr. Locke asked to be shown the house that Mink had occupied. Then he asked for the blankets on which the negro had slept. These could not be found. Well, an old coat would do— anything that the negro had worn or touched. Finally, a dirty, greasy bag, in which Mink had carried his dinner to the field, was found. This would do, Mr. Locke said, and, taking it in his hand, he called his dogs and held it toward them. Sound smelled it more carefully than Music.

"Now, then," said Mr. Locke, "where'bouts was he seed? At the hog-pen last Friday night? All right, we'll ride around there and kinder send him a message."

Joe was very much interested in all this, and he watched Mr. Locke and his dogs very closely. When they arrived at the hog-pen, the negro hunter dismounted and examined the ground. Then he spoke to his dogs.

"Sound!" he exclaimed, sharply, "what are

you doing? Look about.—Music! what are you
here for?"

The shabby little dog seemed to be suddenly transformed. He circled around the hog-
pen rapidly, getting farther and farther away
each time. Mr. Locke never took his eyes
from the dog.

"It's cold—mighty cold," he said, presently.
Then he spoke to the dog again. "Sound!
come here, sir! Now git down to your knit-
ting! Come, knuckle down! Try 'em, old
fellow! try 'em!"

Thus encouraged, the dog, with his nose to
the ground, went carefully around the hog-pen.
At one spot he paused, went on, and then came
back to it. This performance he repeated
several times, and then began to work his way
toward an old field, going very slowly and carefully.

"Well, sir," said Mr. Locke, heaving a sigh
of relief, "I thought it was a gone case, but the
nigger's been here, and we've got him."

"May be the dog is trailing somebody else,"
Joe Maxwell suggested.

Mr. Locke laughed softly and pityingly.
"Why, I tell you what, buddy," he exclaimed,

"if all the niggers in the country had tramped around here that dog wouldn't track none of 'em but the special nigger we're after. Look at that puppy, how he's working!"

And truly it was an interesting if not a beautiful sight to see the dog untangling the tangle of scent. More than once he seemed to be dissatisfied with himself and made little excursions in search of a fresher clew, but he always returned to the point where he had left off, taking up the faint thread of scent and carrying it farther away from the hog-pen. The patience and industry of the dog were marvelous. Mr. Locke himself was patient. He encouraged the hound with his voice, but made no effort to urge him on.

"It's colder than a gravestone," said Mr. Locke, finally. "It's been a long time sence that nigger stepped around here. And the ground's high and dry. If we can work the trail to the branch yonder, he's our meat.—Try for 'im, Sound! Try for 'im."

Gradually the dog worked out the problem of the trail. Across the hill he went, with many turnings and twistings, until finally he struck into the path that led from the negro quarters to the spring where the washing was done. Down this path the hound ran without deigning to put his nose to the ground. At the branch he lapped his fill of water, and then took up his problem again. A half-dozen wash-pots were scattered around, and under the largest a fire was smoldering. On a bench, side by side, three tubs were sitting, and it was at this bench that Sound picked up the trail again. Evidently Mink had paused to chat with the woman who was washing. The ground was moist, and the dog had little trouble. As he recovered the trail he expressed his gratification by a little whimper. The trail led down the spring branch and into a plantation road, then over a fence and across a " new ground " until it struck a bypath that led to an arbor near a church, where the negroes had been holding a revival meeting. At this point there was another problem for the dog. A hundred or two negroes had been gathered here, and it was evident that Mink had been one of the crowd, mingling with the others and walking about with them.

Young Gaither called Mr. Locke's attention to this. " You'll never get the trail away from here in the world," said he. "Why don't you take the dog and circle round with him?"

"That dog," said Mr. Locke, watching the hound anxiously, "has got notions of his own, and he's bound to carry 'em out. He won't be fooled with. Don't say nothing. Just stand off and watch him. He's been in worse places than this here."

But it was a tedious task the dog had before him. Winding in and out in the mazes of an invisible labyrinth, turning and twisting, now slowly, now more rapidly, he pursued with un-erring nose the footsteps of the runaway, and when he had followed the trail away from the church he was going at a brisk pace, and his whimper had changed to an occasional yelp. Mr. Locke, who up to this time had been lead-ing his horse, now took off his coat, folded it carefully, and laid it on his saddle. Then he remounted his horse, and with Gaither and Joe Maxwell trotted along after his dog.

Mink must have lingered on the way, for a quarter of a mile farther on Music joined Sound in his work, and the two dogs footed it along right merrily, their mellow voices rous-ing a hundred echoes among the old red hills.

A mile farther the dogs paused at a tree where there were traces of fire. Scattered around were scraps of sweet-potato peelings and bread.

"Here is where the gentleman roosted last night," said Mr. Locke; and it must have been true, for Sound, with his head in the air, made a half circle, picked up a warmer trail, and the two dogs were off like the wind. Joe Maxwell became very much interested. The horse he was riding was swift and game, and he drew away from the others easily. Neither ditches nor gullies were in his way, and in the excitement a six-rail fence seemed to be no obstacle. Mr. Locke shouted something at Joe, probably some word of warning, but the meaning failed to reach the lad's ears. Butterfly fought for his head and got it, and in the twinkling of an eye carried his rider out of hearing of his companions.

The dogs had swerved a little to the left, and were making straight for the river—the Oconee. Butterfly ran into a plantation road and would have crossed it, but Joe held him to it, and soon discovered that he was gaining on the dogs. From slightly different directions the hounds and the horse seemed to be making

for the same point—and this point, as it turned
out, was the plantation ferry, where a bateau
was kept. Joe Maxwell reached the top of the
hill overlooking the river just as the dogs
reached the ferry. Here he drew rein and
looked about him. The hounds ran about on
the river-bank barking and howling. Sound
went into the water, but, finding that he was
drifting down instead of going across, he made
his way out and shook himself, but still continued to bark. A quarter of a mile away there
was a great bend in the river. Far down this
bend Joe could see a bateau drifting. As he
watched it the thought struck him that it did
not sit as lightly in the water as an empty boat
should. "Suppose," he asked himself, with a
laugh—"suppose Mink is in the bottom of that
bateau?"

He dismissed the thought as Mr. Locke and
young Gaither came up.

"That's a thundering slick hoss you're riding," said Mr. Locke. "He'd do fine work in a
fox-hunt. Where's the nigger?"

"The dogs can tell you more about it than I
can," said Joe.

"Well," remarked Mr. Locke, with a sigh,

"I know'd I'd miss him if he ever got to the ferry here and found the boat on this side. Why, dang his black skin!" exclaimed the negro-hunter vehemently, as he glanced down the river and saw the bateau floating away in the distance, " he's gone and turned the boat loose! That shows we was a-pushin' 'im mighty close. I reckon you could a' seed 'im if you'd looked clos't when you first come up."

"No," replied Joe; "he was out of sight, and the boat was drifting around the elbow. You were not more than five minutes behind me."

"Bless your soul, buddy," exclaimed Mr. Locke, "five minutes is a mighty long time when you are trying to ketch a runaway."

So ended the race after Mink. To Joe Maxwell it was both interesting and instructive. He was a great lover of dogs, and the wonderful performance of Sound had given him new ideas of their sagacity.

A few mornings after the unsuccessful attempt to catch Mink, a very queer thing happened. Harbert was sweeping out the printing-office, picking up the type that had been dropped on the floor, and Joe was preparing to begin the day's work. Suddenly Harbert spoke:

"Marse Joe," said he, "when you rid out ter de river Sunday, is you happen ter see er bateau floatin' 'roun'?"

Joe looked at Harbert for some explanation of the singular question, but the negro pretended to be very busily engaged in picking up scraps of paper.

"Yes," said Joe, after a pause, "I saw a boat drifting down the river. What about it?"

"Well, suh, I speck ef de trufe waz ter git out, dat dey wuz one er yo' ole 'quaintance in dat boat, an' I bet a thrip dat ef you'd a-hollered howdy, dey'd a-hollered howdy back."

Harbert was still too busy to look up.

"Hit de funniest boat what I yever come 'cross," he went on, "agwine floatin' long down by itse'f, an' den, on top er dat, come floatin' long back agin."

"How do you know about the bateau?"

"Whiles you bin gwine 'long de road, Marse Joe," said Harbert, still making a great pretense of gathering up the trash in the room, "ain't you never is see all dem little birds flyin' 'mongst de bushes an' 'long de fence? Well,

suh, dem little birds kin tell mo' tales ef you
listen at 'em right close dan all deze yer papers

"Hit make me dribble at de mouf."

what you bin printin'. Dey er mighty cu'us,

an' dey er mighty cunnin'. Dey tole me lots
mo' dan dat. Dey say dat de young Gaither
boy took an' sont word ter Marse Tom Clemmons dat somebody done gone an' stole de
bateau at de ferry, but yit when Marse Tom go
out fer ter look atter his boat dar she is right
spang whar he lef' 'er. Now, how you 'count
fer dat?"

"Then, Mink—"

"Coon an' 'possum!" interrupted Harbert,
as Mr. Snelson appeared in the doorway.

"'Possum it is!" exclaimed that genial gentleman. "In season or out of season, I'll never
refuse it."

"Well, suh," said Harbert, "ef de talk gwine
ter fall on 'possum, I'm bleeds ter go, kase when
I hear folks talkin' 'bout 'possum hit make me
dribble at de mouf." The negro went off laughing loudly.

CHAPTER IV.

SHADOWS OF THE WAR.

WHAT with the books in the library and the life out of doors in the afternoons, Joe Maxwell grew very fond of his new home. His work at the printers' case was not a task, but a pleasure. He grew to be an expert in type-setting and won unstinted praise from Mr. Snelson. Sometimes he wrote little paragraphs of his own, crediting them to " The Countryman's Devil," and the editor was kind enough to make no objection, and this fact was very encouraging to the lad, who was naturally shy and sensitive.

Only the echoes of the war were heard at the Turner place ; but once the editor returned from Hillsborough with some very sad news for a lady who lived near *The Countryman* office with her father. Her husband had been killed in one of the great battles, and her screams when the editor told her of it, and the cries of

her little daughter, haunted Joe Maxwell for
many a long day. Sometimes he lay awake at
night thinking about it, and out of the darkness
it seemed to him that he could build a grim
mirage of war, vanishing and reappearing like
an ominous shadow, and devouring the people.

The war was horrible enough, distant as it
was, but the people who were left at home—the
women and children, the boys, the men who
were exempt, the aged and the infirm—had
fears of a fate still more terrible. They were
fears that grew out of the system of slavery,
and they grew until they became a fixed habit
of the mind. They were the fears of a negro in-
surrection. The whites who were left at home
knew that it was in the power of the negroes to
rise and in one night sweep the strength and
substance of the Southern Confederacy from
the face of the earth. Some of the more ignorant whites lived in constant terror.

Once it was whispered around that the blacks
were preparing to rise, and the fears of the people were so ready to confirm the rumor that the
plantations were placed in a state of siege.
The patrol—called by the negroes "patter-
rollers"—was doubled, and for a time the negro

quarters in all parts of the country were visited
nightly by the guard. But Joe Maxwell noticed
that the patrol never visited the Turner plantation, and he learned afterward that they had
been warned off. The editor of *The Countryman*
had the utmost confidence in his negroes, and
he would not allow them to be disturbed at
night by the "patter-rollers." He laughed at
the talk of a negro uprising, and it was a
favorite saying of his that the people who
treated their negroes right had nothing to fear
from them.

As for Joe Maxwell, he had no time to think
about such things. He sometimes rode with
the patrol on their fruitless and sometimes foolish errands, but his curiosity with regard to
them was soon satisfied, and he was better con-
tented when he was spending his evenings at
home with his books, or in listening to the
wonderful tales that Mr. Snelson told for his
benefit. In spite of the fact that his work in
the little printing-office was confining, the lad
managed to live an outdoor life for a good part
of the time. He had a task to do—so many
thousand ems to set—and then he was through
for the day. The thoughtful Mr. Snelson added

to this task from time to time, but Joe always managed to complete it so as to have the greater part of the afternoon for his own.

There was a hat-shop on the plantation presided over by Mr. Wall, a queer old man from North Carolina. With the thrift of youth Joe gave the amusement of rabbit-hunting a business turn. In the fall and winter, when the rabbits were in fur, their skins could be sold at the hat-shop at twenty-five cents a dozen, and the little harriers were so industrious and so well trained that he sometimes sold as many as three dozen skins a week. In addition to the pleasure and the money he got from the sport, he became very much interested in the hat-shop.

The hats were made as they had been during the Revolution, and as they were no doubt made in England before the Revolution. The hair on the pelts or skins was scraped off with a knife fashioned like a shoemaker's knife. The fur was then cut away with a steel blade that had no handle. When there was enough fur to make a hat it was placed on a bench or counter. Over the counter was suspended a long staff, to which was fastened a bowstring. If the staff

Joe returns from a rabbit hunt.

had been bent it would have had the appearance of a huge bow, but it was straight, and the rawhide string was allowed a little play. With an instrument not unlike a long spool the hatter would catch the bowstring, pull it away from the staff, and allow it to whip against the fur as it sprang back into place. This whipping was carried on very rapidly, and was kept up until every tuft of fur was broken apart. Then the fur was whipped gently into what was called a bat, shaped somewhat like a section of orange peel. The hatter then spread a cambric cloth carefully over it, pressed it down a little, seized the cloth in the middle between thumb and forefinger, gave it a flirt in the air and lifted fur and all. To Joe Maxwell it seemed like a trick of magic.

The cloth, with the bat of fur lying smoothly and neatly in its fold, was then placed on a heating box, and kneaded rapidly but gently. When it seemed to be getting too hot it was sprinkled with water. This kneading was kept up until the fur shrunk together. When taken from the cloth it was in the shape of the hats the clowns used to wear in the circus, and it was called a bonnet. The bonnet was then

dipped in boiling water and pressed and kneaded with an instrument shaped like a rolling-pin,
but smaller. The workers in this department
were compelled to protect their hands from the
boiling water by means of leather fastened to
the palms of their hands. The more the bonnets
were rolled and kneaded, the more they shrunk,
until finally they were ready to be placed on
the blocks that gave them the hat shape. They
were fitted to these blocks, which were of
various sizes, and thrown into a caldron of boiling water, where they were allowed to stay
until they would shrink no more.

When hats became scarce after the breaking
out of the war, the editor bought Mr. Wall's interest in the hat-shop, and made him foreman.
Several negroes were placed under him, and
they soon became experts in hat-making. There
was a great demand for the hats from all over
the South, and on one occasion Joe Maxwell
sold a dozen wool hats for $500—in Confederate
money.

But the most interesting thing about the
shop, as Joe thought, was the head hatter, Miles
Wall, who was the quaintest old man that Joe
had ever seen. He was illiterate—he didn't

know a letter in the book—and yet he was not
ignorant.   The Bible had been read to him
until he was grounded in its texts and teachings,
and he was always ready for an argument on
politics or religion.

He was always ready for an argument.

"Whenever you hear anybody a-axing anything," he used to say, " 'bout how I'm a-gettin'
on, an' how my family is, un' whether er no my
health is well, you thess up an' tell um that I'm
a nachul Baptis'.   You thess up an' tell um that,
an' I'll be mighty much erbleege to you.   Tell
um I'm a born'd Baptis'."

Although Mr. Wall was unable to read or write, Joe Maxwell found him to be a very interesting talker. Perhaps it was his ignorance of books that made him interesting. He was more superstitious than any of the negroes—a great believer in signs and omens. One night when Joe went to visit him, the old man told a story that made a very deep impression on the lad. There was nothing in the story, but Mr. Wall identified himself with it, and told it in a way that made it seem real, and it was a long time before Joe could divest himself of the idea that the story was not true. Wherever Mr. Wall got it, whether he dreamed it or heard it, there is no doubt that he really believed it.

CHAPTER V.

MR. WALL'S STORY.

THIS is the way he told it, by the light of a pine-knot fire that threw a wavering and an uncertain light over the little room :

"I'm monst'us sorry Daught ain't here," he began, "'cause she know'd the folks thess ez well ez I did; she's been thar at the house an' seed um. It thess come inter my min' whilst we been a-settin' here talkin' 'bout ghostses an' the like er that. Daught's over yander settin' up wi' Miss Clemmons, an' I wisht she wuz here. She know'd 'em all.

"Well, sir, it wuz in North Ca'liny, right nex' ter the Ferginny line, whar we all cum frum. They wuz a fammerly thar by the name er Chambliss—Tom Chambliss an' his wife—an' they had a boy name John, in about ez peart a chap ez you ever set your eyes on. Arter awhile, Miss Chambliss, she took sick an' died.

Tom, he moped aroun' right smartually, but
'twan't long fo' he whirled in an' married agin.
He went away off some'rs for to get his wife,
the Lord knows whar, an' she wuz a honey!
She fussed so much an' went on so that Tom,
he took ter drink, an' he went from dram ter
dram tell he wern't no manner account. Then
she took arter John, the boy, an' she thess made
that child's life miserbul a-doggin' arter him all
day long an' half the night.

"One Sunday she fixed up an' went ter
church, arter tellin' Johnny for to stay at home
an' keep the chickens outn' the sallid-patch.
She locked the door of the house before she
went off an' took the key wi' 'er. It wuz right
down coolish, but the sun wuz a-shinin' an'
Johnny didn't min' the cold. Ther' wuz a big
white oak-tree in the yard, an' he clum' up that
an' crope out on a lim' an' got on top er the
house, an' sot up thar a-straddle er the comb.
He wuz a feeling mighty lonesome, an' he
didn't know what ter do wi' hisse'f skacely.

"I dunno how long he sot thar, but presently
a great big acorn dropped on the roof—*ker-
bang!* It wuz sech a big one an' it fell so hard
that it made Johnny jump. It fell on the roof

'bout half-way betwixt the comb an' the eaves,
an' when Johnny looked aroun' for to see what
made the fuss he seed the acorn a-rollin' up
to'rds whar he wuz a-settin'. Yes, sir! stedder
rollin' down the roof an' fallin' off on the groun',
the acorn come a-rollin' up the shingles thess
like it wuz down grade. Johnny grabbed it ez
it come. He picked it up an' looked at it good,
an' then turned it roun' an' 'roun' for to see
what kinder consarn it wuz that rolled up hill
stedder rollin' down hill. While he wuz a
turnin' the acorn aroun' he spied a worm hole in
it, an' he was thess about ter break it open when
he heard somebody callin'. It sounded like his
stepmammy wuz a-callin' 'im from a way off
yander, an' he answered back 'Ma'am!' thess
ez loud as ever he could, an' then he sot still an'
listened. Bimeby he heard the callin' again,
an' he answered back: 'Who is you, an' whar
is you?' It seemed like then that he could
hear somebody laughin' at 'im some'rs. These
here sounds sorter put 'im out, an' he took an'
shot the acorn down the roof like it wuz a
marvel. Yit, before it could fall off, it seemed
ter kinder ketch itself, an' then it come a-rollin'
back to Johnny.

"This sorter made Johnny feel kinder creepy. He know'd mighty well that he didn't have no loadstone in his pocket, an' he couldn't make no head ner tail to sech gwine's on. He picked up the acorn an' looked at it closeter than ever, an' turned it 'roun' an' 'roun' in his hand, an' helt it right up to his eye. Whilst he was a-holdin' it up that a-way he heard a little bit er voice ez fine ez a cambric needle, an' it seem like it wuz a-singin':

> "Ningapie, Ningapie!
> Why do you hol' me at your eye?
> Ningapie, Ningapee!
> Don't you know that you can't see?
> Ningapie, Ningapeer!
> Why don't you hol' me to your ear?

"Johnny didn't know whether to laugh er cry, but he helt the acorn to his ear, an' he heard sumpin' er other on the inside holler out:

"'Why don't you hold my house so I can talk out'n my window?'

"'I don't see no window,' says Johnny, sorter shakin' a little, bekase the Watchermacollum talked like it was mad. 'Is thish here wormhole your window?'

"'Tooby shore it is,' say the Whatshisname,

'it's my window an' my front door, an' my peazzer.'

" ' Why, it ain't bigger than the pint of a pin,' says Johnny.

"He helt the acorn to his ear."

" ' But ef it wuzn't big enough,' say the—er —Watchermacollum, ' I'd make it bigger.'

" ' What is your name?' says Johnny.

" ' Ningapie.'

" ' It's a mighty funny name,' says Johnny. ' Where did you come from?'

" ' Chuckalucker town.'

" ' That's in the song,' says Johnny.

"'Me, too,' says Ningapie. 'It's in the song. Ain't you never heard it?'

> "Ningapie! Ningapan!
> He up an' killed the Booger Man!
> Ningapie, Ningapitch!
> 'He's the one to kill a witch.'

"Johnny wuz so took up wi' the talkin' an' the singin' of the little feller in the acorn that he didn't hear his stepmammy when she come, an' when he did hear her he wuz that skeered that he shook like a poplar-leaf.

"'Watch out!' says the little chap in the acorn. 'Watch out! Be right still. Don't move. I want to show you sumpin'.'

"'She'll skin me alive,' says Johnny.

"'Thess wait,' says the little chap. 'If she calls you, keep right still.'

"Mis. Chambliss onlocked the door an' went in the house, an' slammed things down like she wuz mad. She flung the tongs down on the h'ath, slung the shovel in a corner, an' sot a cheer back like she wuz tryin' for to drive it thoo the wall. Then she began to jaw.

"'I'll get 'im! Me a-tellin' 'im to stay an' min' the sallid-patch, an' he a-runnin' off! Won't I make 'im pay for it?'

" ' That's me,' says Johnny, an' he talked like he wuz mighty nigh ready to cry.

" ' Thess wait! ' says the little chap in the acorn. ' Keep right still! '

" Bimeby Mis. Chambliss come out'n the house an' looked all aroun'. Then she called Johnny. She had a voice like a dinner-horn, an' you moughter heard her a mile or more. Johnny he shook an' shivered, but he stayed still. His stepmammy called an' called, an' looked ever'whar for Johnny exceptin' in the right place. Then she went back in the house an' presently she come out. She had a little spade in one hand an' a little box in t' other.

" ' Watch her! ' says the little chap in the acorn. ' Keep your eye on her! '

" She went down in the gyarden an' walked along tell she come to a Mogul plum-tree, an' then she knelt down an' begun to dig away at the roots of it. She dug an' dug, and then she put the box in the hole an' covered it up.

" ' Oho! ' says the little chap in the acorn. ' Now you see whar she hides her money an' your daddy's money. Ever'body thinks your daddy has been a-throwin' his money away, an' thar's whar it's gone. I've been a-watchin' her a long time.'

"'I ain't botherin' 'bout the money,' says Johnny. 'I'm a-thinkin' 'bout the frailin' I'm gwine to git.'

"'Well,' says the little chap in the acorn, 'when she goes to the spring for to fetch a bucket of water, put me in your pocket an' climb down from here. Then go up the road a piece, an' there you'll see a red cow a-grazin'. Walk right up to her, slap her on the back, an' say, "Ningapie wants you." Fetch her home an' tell your stepmammy that a stranger told you that you might have her ef you'd go an' git her.'

"Shore enough, 'twan't long before Mis. Chambliss come out'n the house an' started to the spring for to git a bucket of water. She had done took an' pulled off her Sunday-go-to-meetin' duds, an' she looked mighty scrawny in her calico frock. Time she got out'n sight Johnny put the acorn in his pocket an' scrambled down to the groun', an' then he split off up the road ez hard ez ever he could go. He didn't go so mighty fur before he seed a red cow feedin' by the side of the road, an' she wuz

a fine cow, too, ez fat ez a butter-ball, an' lookin'
like she mought be able for to give four gallons
of milk a day an' leave some over for the calf
wharsoever the calf mought be. When she
seed Johnny walkin' right to'rds her, she raised
her head an' sorter blowed like cow creeturs
will do, but she stood stock still tell Johnny
come up an' patted her on the back an' says:

" ' Ningapie wants you.'

" Then she shook her head an' trotted along
at Johnny's heels, an' Johnny marched down
the road a-swellin' up wi' pride tell he like to
bust the buttons off'n his coat. When he got
home his stepmammy wuz a-stan'in' at the gate
a-waitin' for him wi' a hickory, but when she
seed the cow a-followin' long behine him, she
took an' forgot all about the whippin' she'd laid
up.

" ' Why, Johnny!' say she, 'whar in the
wide world did you git sech a be-u-tiful
cow?'"

In his effort to mimic a woman's voice, Mr.
Wall screwed up his mouth and twisted it
around to such an alarming extent that Joe
Maxwell thought for an instant the old man was
going to have a spasm. The lad laughed so

heartily when he found out his mistake that Mr.
Wall repeated his effort at mimicking.

"'Why, Johnny,' say she, 'whar in the wide
world did you git sech a be-u-tiful cow?'

"Johnny, he up an' tol' his stepmammy
what Ningapie tol' 'im to say, an' the ole 'oman,
she wuz e'en about ez proud ez Johnny wuz.
She patted the cow on the back, an' muched
her up might'ly, an' then she took her in the
lot an' got ready fer to milk her. Johnny felt
the acorn a-jumpin' about in his pocket, an' he
took it out an' helt it up to his ear.

"'Watch her when she goes to milk,' says
Ningapie.

"Johnny clumb the fence an' waited. Thess
'bout the time his stepmammy begun fer to
milk the cow good, a little black dog come
a-rushin' 'roun' the yard a-barkin' fit to kill.
Time she heard 'im, the cow give a jump an'
come mighty nigh knockin' ole Mis. Chambliss
over. Time everything got quiet, here come a
big pack of dogs a-chargin' 'roun' the lot-palin's
in full cry, an' it look like to Johnny that the
cow would shorely have a fit.

"When night come," Mr. Wall continued,
throwing another pine-knot into the fire,

"Johnny got some milk for his supper, an' then he went to bed. He helt the acorn to his ear for to tell the little chap good-night.

"'Don't put me on the shelf,' says Ningapie, 'an' don't put me on the floor.'

"'Why?' says Johnny, in a whisper.

"'Bekaze the rats might git me,' says Ningapie.

"'Well,' says Johnny, 'I'll let you sleep on my piller.'

"Some time in the night Johnny felt sump'n run across the foot of his bed. He wuz wide awake in a minit, but he kept mighty still, bekaze he wuz skeer'd. Presently he felt sump'n jump up on his bed an' run across it. Then it popped in his head about Ningapie, an' he felt for the acorn tell he found it.

"'Now's your time,' says Ningapie. "Git up an' put on your clozes quick an' foller the little black dog.'

"Johnny jumped up, an' was ready in three shakes of a sheep's tail, an' he could hear the little black dog a-caperin' aroun' on the floor. When he started, he took the acorn in his han'. The door opened to let him out, an' shot itse'f when he got out, an' then the little black dog went trottin' down the big road. It wuz dark, but the stars wuz a-shinin', an' Johnny could tell by the ell-an'-yard " (the constellation of Orion) " that it wuz nigh midnight.

" They hadn't gone fur before they come to a big white hoss a-standin' in the road, chompin' his bit an' pawin' the groun'.

" ' Mount the hoss,' says Ningapie.

" Johnny jumped on his back, an' the hoss went canterin' down the road. 'Twan't long 'fore Johnny seed a light shinin' in the road, an' when he got a little nigher he seed it was right in the middle of the cross roads. A fire was a-blazin' up thar, an' who should be a-feedin' of it but his stepmammy? Her hair wuz a-hangin' down, an' she looked like ole Nick hisse'f. She wuz a-walkin' 'roun' the blaze, a-mumblin' some kinder talk, an' a-makin' motions wi' her han's, an' thar wuz a great big black cat a-walkin' 'roun' wi' her, an' a-rubbin' up agin her, and the creetur's tail wuz swelled up out'n all reason.

" ' Watch out, now,' says Ningapie, ' an' hold on to your hoss.'

" He hadn't more'n spoke the words before a pack of dogs broke out of the woods an' made

right for the ole 'oman, an' Johnny's hoss a-fol-
lerin' 'em. Thar wuz a monst'us scatteration of
chunks an' fire-coals, an' then it looked like
'oman, dogs, an' all riz up in the elements, an'
thar wuz sech another yowlin' an' howlin' an'
growlin' ez ain't never been heard in them parts
before nor sence.

"When Johnny got back home he found his
pappy a-waitin' for.him, an' he looked like a new
man. Then they went down into the gyarden,
an' thar they foun' a pile of gold packed up in
little boxes. Ez for the ole 'oman, she never
did come back. She wuz a witch, an' Ningapie
unwitched her."

"And what become of the acorn?" asked
Joe Maxwell.

"Ah, Lord!" said Mr. Wall, with a sigh,
"you know how boys is. Like ez not, Johnny
took an' cracked it open wi' a hammer for to
see what kind of a creetur Ningapie wuz."

CHAPTER VI.

THE OWL AND THE BIRDS.

THE Gaither boy grew to be very friendly with Joe Maxwell, and he turned out to be a very pleasant companion. He was fifteen years old, but looked younger, and although he had no book-learning, he was very intelligent, having picked up a great deal of the wholesome knowledge that Nature keeps in store for those who make her acquaintance. He could read a little, and he could write his name, which he took great pride in doing, using a stick for a pen and a bed of sand for a copy-book. Walking along through the fields or woods, he would pause wherever the rains had washed the sand together, and write his name in full in letters that seemed to be wrestling with each other—"James K. Polk Gaither." As there was another James in his family, he was called Jim-Polk Gaither.

His friendship was worth a great deal to Joe Maxwell, for there was not a bird in the woods nor a tree that he did not know the name of and something of its peculiarities, and he was familiar with every road and bypath in all the country around. He knew where the wild strawberries grew, and the chincapins and chestnuts, and where the muscadines, or, as he called them, the "bullaces," were ripest. The birds could not hide their nests from him, nor the wild creatures escape him. He had a tame buzzard that sometimes followed him about in his rambles. He set traps for flying squirrels, and tamed them as soon as his hands touched them. He handled snakes fearlessly, and his feats with them were astounding to the town lad until Joe discovered that the serpents were not of the poisonous species. In handling highland moccasins and spreading adders, Jim-Polk confined his feats to seizing them by their tails as they ran and snapping their heads off. Whenever he killed one in this way he always hung it on a bush or tree in order, as he said, to bring rain. When it failed to rain, his explanation was that as a snake never dies until sundown, no matter how early in the morning it may be killed, it had twisted and writhed until it fell from the limb or bush on which it was hung.

Jim-Polk had many gifts and acquirements that interested Joe Maxwell. Once when the two lads were walking through the woods they saw a pair of hawks some distance away. Jim-Polk motioned to Joe to hide under a hawthorn bush. Then, doubling his handkerchief before his mouth, he began to make a curious noise—a series of smothered exclamations that sounded like hoo!—hoo!—hoo-hoo! He was imitating the cry of the swamp owl, which Joe Maxwell had never heard. The imitation must have been perfect, for immediately there was a great commotion in the woods. The smaller birds fluttered away and disappeared; but the two hawks, re-enforced by a third, came flying toward the noise with their feathers ruffled and screaming with indignation. They meant war. Jim - Polk continued his muffled cries, until presently the boys heard a crow cawing in the distance.

" Now you'll see fun," said young Gaither. " Just keep right still."

The crow was flying high in the air, and

would have gone over but the muffled cry of
the owl—hoo! hoo! hoo! hoo!—caught its ear
and it paused in its flight, alighting in the top
of a tall pine. Swinging in this airy outlook, it
sent forth its hoarse signals, and in a few minutes the pine was black with its companions, all
making a tremendous outcry. Some of them
dropped down into the tops of the scrub-oaks.
They could not find the owl, but they caught
sight of the hawks, and sounded their war-cry.
Such cawing, screaming, fluttering, and fight-
ing Joe Maxwell had never seen before. The
hawks escaped from the crows, but they left
many of their feathers on the battle-field. One
of the hawks did not wholly escape, for in his
fright he flew out of the woods into the open,
and there he was pounced on by a kingbird,
which Jim-Polk called a bee martin. This little
bird, not larger than his cousin, the catbird, lit
on the hawk's back and stayed there as long as
they remained in sight. The commotion set up
by the crows had attracted the attention of all
the birds, except the smallest, and they flew
about in the trees, uttering notes of anger or
alarm, all trying to find the owl.

The incident was very interesting to Joe

Maxwell. He discovered that the owl is the winged Ishmael of the woods, the most hated and most feared of all the birds. A few days afterward he went with Harbert to see the hogs fed, and he told the negro how all the birds seemed to hate the owl.

"Lord! yes, sah!" said Harbert, who seemed to know all about the matter. "Ain't you never is hear tell er de tale 'bout de owl an' de yuther birds? Ole man Remus tole it ter me dis many a year ago, an' sence den I bin hear talk about it mo' times dan what I got fingers an' toes."

Of course, Joe wanted to hear—

THE STORY OF THE OWL.

"Well, suh," said Harbert, "hit run sorter like dis: One time way back yander, fo' ole man Remus wuz born'd, I speck, all de birds wuz in cahoots; dem what fly in de air, an' dem what walk on de groun', an' dem what swim on de water—all un um. Dey all live in one settlement, an' whatsomever dey mought pick up endurin' er de day, dey'd fetch it ter der place wharbouts dey live at, an' put it wid de rest what de yuther ones bin a-ketchin' an' a-fetchin'.

Dey kep' on dis away, twel, twant long fo' dey
done save up a right smart pile er fust one
thing an' den anudder. De pile got so big dat
dey 'gun ter git skeered dat some un 'ud come
'long whilst dey wus away an' he'p derse'f.
Bimeby some er de mo' 'spicious 'mong um up
an' say dat somebody bin stealin' fum de pro-
vision what dey savin' up ginst hard times. Mr.
Jaybird, he coyspon' wid Mr. Crow, an' Mr.
Crow he coyspon' wid Miss Chicken Hawk,
and Miss Chicken Hawk she coyspon' wid Mr.
Eagle, which he was de big buckra er all de
birds. An' den dey all coyspon' wid one
anudder, an' dey 'low dat dey bleeze ter lef'
somebody dar fer ter watch der winter wittles
whiles dey er off a-huntin' up mo'. Dey jowered
an' jowered a long time, twel, bimeby, Mr.
Eagle, he up an' say dat de bes' dey kin do is to
'pint Mr. Owl fer ter keep watch. Mr. Owl he
sorter hoot at dis, but 'tain't do no good, kaze
de yuthers, dey say dat all Mr. Owl got ter do
is ter sleep mo' endurin' er de night an' stay
'wake endurin' er de day.

"So, den," Harbert went on, pausing as if
trying to remember the thread of the story,
" dey 'pinted Mr. Owl fer ter keep watch, an'

dey all flewd off, some one way an' some anudder. Mr. Owl, he tuck his seat, he did, whar
he kin take in a right smart stretch er country
wid his big eyeball, an' he sot dar right peart.
But bimeby he 'gun ter git lonesome. Dey
want nobody ter talk ter, an' de sun shine so
bright dat he bleeze ter shet his eye, an' 'fo' he
know what he doin' he wuz a settin' dar noddin'
same ez a nigger by a hick'ry fire. Every once
in a while he'd ketch hissef an' try ter keep
'wake, but, do what he would, he can't keep his
eye open, an' bimeby he snap his mouf like
he mad an' den he slapped his head under his
wing an' dropped off ter sleep good fashion.
Kaze when a bird git his head under his wing
hit's des de same ez gwine ter bed an' pullin' de
kiver 'roun' yo' years.

"Well, suh, dar he wuz, settin' up fast asleep.
'Long in de co'se er de day, Mr. Crow an' Mr.
Jaybird, dey struck up wid one annuder out in
de woods, an' dey sot down in a popular-tree
fer to carry on a confab. Dey done bin coyspon' wid one anudder an' dey bofe bin pullin'
up corn. Mr. Crow 'low ter Mr. Jaybird dat he
ain't so mighty certain an' shore 'bout Mr. Owl,
kaze he mighty sleepy-headed. Wid dat, Mr.

Jaybird, he up an' say dat he got dat ve'y idee in his min'. Dey sot dar an' swop talk 'bout Mr. Owl, twel, atter while, dey 'gree ter go back fer de settlement an' see what Mr. Owl doin'.

"Well, suh, dey went dar, an' dar dey foun' 'im. Yasser! Mr. Owl sholy wuz dar. He wuz settin' up on a lim' wid his head flung under his wing, an' 'twuz all dey kin do fer ter wake 'im up. Dey hollered at 'im des loud ez dey kin, an' bimeby he woke up an' tuck his head out from under his wing an' look at um des ez sollum ez a camp-meetin' preacher. Dey 'buze 'im—dey quoiled—dey call 'im out'n his name—dey jowered at 'im—but tain't do no good. He des sot dar, he did, an' look at um, an' he ain't say nuthin' 'tall. Dis make Mr. Crow an' Mr. Jaybird mighty mad, kaze when folks quoil an' can't git nobody for ter quoil back at um, it make um wusser mad dan what dey wuz at fust. Dat night when de yuther birds come home, Mr. Crow an' Mr. Jaybird, dey had a mighty tale ter tell. Some b'lieved um an' some didn't b'lieve um. Miss Jenny Wren, an' Mr. Jack Sparrow, an' Miss Cat Bird, dey b'lieved um, an' dey went on so twel de yuther birds can't hear der own years, skacely. But de big

birds, dey sorter helt off, an' say dey gwine ter
give Mr. Owl anudder chance.

" Well, suh, dey give Mr. Owl two mo' trials,
let alone one, an' eve'y time dey lef' 'im dar fer
ter watch an' gyard, dey'd fin' 'im fast asleep.

" He des sot dar, he did, an' look at um."

An' dat ain't all; dey skivered dat somebody
done bin slippin' in an' totin' off der provisions.
Dat settle de hash fer Mr. Owl.   De birds sot a
day an' fotch Mr. Owl up fer ter stan' trial, an'
dey laid down de law dat fum dat time forrud
dat Mr. Owl shan't go wid de yuther birds, an'

dat de nex' time dey kotch 'im out de word wuz
ter be give, an' dey wuz all ter fall foul un 'im
an' frail 'm out. Den dey say dat when he sleep
he got ter sleep wid bofe eyes wide open, a'n
dey lay it down dat he got ter keep watch all
night long, an' dat whensomever he hear any
fuss he got ter holler out :

"'Who—who—who pesterin' we all?'

"Dat de way de law stan's," continued Harbert, placing his basket of corn on the top rail
of the fence, "an dat de way it gwine ter stan'.
Down ter dis day, when Mr. Owl asleep, he
sleep wid his eye wide open, an' when de
yuther birds ketch him out, dey light on to 'im
like folks puttin' out fire, an' when he ups an'
hollers in de night-time, you kin hear 'im say:

"'Who—who—who pesterin' we all?'"

With a laugh, in which Joe Maxwell heartily
joined Harbert turned his attention to calling
his hogs, and the way he did this was as interesting to Joe as the story had been. He had a
voice of wonderful strength and power, as pene-
trating and as melodious as the notes of a
cornet. On a still day, when there was a little
moisture in the air, Harbert could make himself heard two miles. The range over which

the hogs roamed was at least a mile and a half from the pen. In calling them the negro broke into a song. It was only the refrain that the distant hogs could hear, but as it went echoing over the hills and valleys it seemed to Joe to be the very essence of melody. The song was something like this:

HOG-FEEDER'S SONG.

Oh, rise up, my ladies, lissen unter me,
Gwoop! Gwoop! Gee-woop! Goo-whee!
I'm a-gwine dis night fer ter knock along er you.
Gwoop! Gwoop! Gee-woop! Goo-whoo!
Pig-goo! Pig-gee¹ Gee-o-whee!

Oh, de stars look bright des like dey gwineter fall,
En 'way todes sundown you hear de killdee call:
Stee-wee! Killdee! Pig-goo! Pig-gee!
Pig! Pig! Pig-goo! Pig! Pig! Pig-gee!

De blue barrer squeal kaze he can't squeeze froo,
En he hump up he back, des like niggers do—
Oh, humpty-umpty blue! Pig-gee! Pig-goo!
Pig! Pig! Pig-gee! Pig! Pig! Pig-goo!

Oh, rise up, my ladies! ˌLissen unter me!
Gwoop! Gwoopee! Gee-woop! Goo-whee!
I'm a-gwine dis night a gallantin' out wid you!
Gwoop! Gwoopee! Gee-woop! Goo-hoo!
Pig-goo! Pig-gee! Gee-o-whee!

Ole sow got sense des ez sho's youer bo'n
'Kaze she tak'n hunch de baskit fer ter shatter out co'n—
Ma'am, you makes too free! Pig-goo! Pig-gee!
Pig! Pig! Pig-goo! Pig! Pig! Pig-gee!

W'en de pig git fat he better stay close,
'Kaze fat pig nice fer ter hide out en' roas'—
En he taste mighty good in de barbecue!
Oh, roas' pig, shoo! 'N-yum! dat barbecue!
Pig! Pig! Pig-gee! Pig! Pig! Pig-goo!

Oh, rise up, my ladies! Lissen unter me:
Gwoop! Gwoopee! Gee-woop! Goo-whee!
I'm a-gwine dis night fer ter knock aroun' wid you!
Gwoop! Gwoopee! Gee-woop! Goo-whoo!
Pig-goo! Pig-gee! Gee-o-whee!

"Marse Joe," said Harbert, after he had counted the hogs to see that none were missing, "I got sumpin' at my house fer you. I'm layin' off fer ter fetch it dis ve'y night."

"What is it?" asked Joe.

"Tain't much," said Harbert. "Des some 'simmon beer an' some ginger-cake."

"I'm very much obliged to you," said Joe.

"Oh, 'tain't me," said Harbert, quickly. "I was puttin' up de carriage-horses las' night when I hear somebody callin' me, an' I went ter de fence, an' dar wuz a nigger 'oman wid a jug in one han' an' a bundle in de udder, an' she say dar wuz some 'simmon beer an' some ginger-cakes, an' she up an' ax me would I be so compleasant fer to give um ter Marse Joe Maxwell, an' I 'lowed dat I'd be so compleasant."

"Who was the woman?" Joe asked.

"She some kin ter Mink," answered Harbert, evasively.

"Well, what kin?" asked Joe.

"She ain't so mighty much kin, needer," said Harbert. "She des his wife. She 'low dat ef you got any washin' er darnin' dat you want done she be glad ter do it, an' den I say, 'Shoo nigger 'oman! G'way fum here! What you speck my wife here fer?'"

Here Harbert tried to look indignant, but failed. Presently he continued:

"Dat are 'simmon beer got sign in it."

"What sign is that?" asked Joe.

"Well, suh, when 'simmonses is ripe hit's a shore sign dat 'possum ready ter eat, an' tain't gwine ter be long 'fo' you hear me a-hollerin' 'roun' thoo de woods, mo' speshually if I kin git holt er dem dogs what dat Gaither boy got. When it come ter 'possum an' coon dey er de outdoin'est dogs you ever is lay yo' eyes on."

"I can get the dogs any time," said Joe.

"Well, suh," said Harbert with enthusiasm, "atter to-night you can't git um too soon."

CHAPTER VII.

OLD ZIP COON.

JIM-POLK GAITHER was very glad to go hunting with Joe Maxwell, having taken a strong boyish liking to the lad, and so one Saturday evening he came over to the Turner place with his dogs, Jolly and Loud. They were large, fine-looking hounds, and Joe examined them with interest. Their color was black and tan, and each had two little yellow spots over his eyes. Loud was the heavier of the two, and Jim-Polk explained that he had "the best nose" and the best voice, and yet he declared that in some respects Jolly was the best dog.

Harbert had already prepared for the hunt, and he soon made his appearance with an axe and a bundle of fat twine to be used for torches.

"Now, then," said Jim-Polk, "what kind of

game do you want? Shall it be 'possum or coon?"

"Dat's for Marse Joe to say," said Harbert.

"These are mighty funny dogs," explained Jim-Polk. "If you start out wi' a light, they'll hunt 'possums all night long. If you go into the woods an' fetch a whoop or two before you strike a light, they won't notice no 'possum ; but

Old Zip Coon.

you better believe they'll make old Zip Coon lift hisself off'n the ground. So whichever you want you'll have to start out right."

"'Possum mighty good," said Harbert, seeing Joe hesitate.

"Lots of fun in runnin' a coon," said Jim-Polk.

"Well," said Joe, "let's start without a light."

"Dat settles it," exclaimed Harbert, with a good-humored grimace. "I done bin hunt wid deze dogs befo'."

"You must have stole 'em out," said Jim-Polk.

"No, suh," replied Harbert, "I went wid Mink."

"I wish to goodness," exclaimed Jim-Polk, "that Mink was at home. Pap, he sides with the overseer, but when I get a little bigger I'm a-goin' to whirl in and give that overseer a frailin', if it's the last act."

"Now you talkin'!" said Harbert, with emphasis.

It was some time before they got free of the pasture-land, and then they went by Mr. Snelson's, so that Joe might change his clothes for a rougher suit. That genial gentleman was very much interested in the hunt, and he finally persuaded himself to go.

"I'll go," said he, "joost to pertect the lads. It's a fine mess I'm after gettin' into, and it's all

on account of me good feelin's.   They'll be the
death of me some day, and thin a fine man'll be
gone wit' nobuddy to take his place."

Mr. Snelson was so enthusiastic that he
wanted to lead the way, but after he had fallen
over a stump and rushed headlong into a brush-
heap, he was content to give the lead to Harbert.

Jim-Polk, who was bringing up the rear with
Joe Maxwell, gave the latter to understand that
even if they didn't catch a coon, they'd have a
good deal of fun with the genial printer.

"We'll have fun with him," said Jim-Polk,
"if we don't have to tote him home."

Mr. Snelson kept up a running fire of conversation, which was only interrupted when he
stepped into a hole or a ditch.

" I've often read of chasing the raccoon," he
said, "but it never occurred to me mind it was
anything approachin' this.   You're right sure
it's the regular thing ? "

" You'll think so before you get back
home," remarked Jim-Polk.   Harbert, knowing what these words really meant, laughed
loudly.

" Well, well," said the genial printer, "if it's

all a joke, I'd as well turn in me tracks and go home."

"Oh, no!" exclaimed Jim-Polk. "Don't go home. If you think it's a joke when we get through with it, you may have my hat."

"Dat's so," cried Harbert. "Dat's so, sho! An' ef he wuz ter git de hat, I speck I'd ha' ter he'p 'm tote it. Yasser! Dat what I speck."

The enthusiastic Mr. Snelson and Harbert were ahead, and Joe Maxwell and Jim-Polk brought up the rear.

"I hope my dogs'll behave their selves to-night," said young Gaither. "You went on so about Bill Locke's nigger dogs that I want you to hear Jolly and Loud when they get their bristles up. But they're mighty quare. If Loud strikes a trail first, Jolly will begin to pout. I call it poutin'. He'll run along with Loud, but he won't open his mouth until the scent gets hot enough to make him forget himself. If it's a 'possum, he'll let old Loud do all the trailin' and the treein'. You'd think there was only one dog, but when you get to the tree you'll find Jolly settin' there just as natchul as life."

The hunters had now come to the lands bor-

dering on Rocky Creek, and, even while Jim-
Polk was speaking, the voice of a dog was
heard. Then it was twice repeated—a mellow,
far-reaching, inspiring sound, that caused every
nerve in Joe Maxwell's body to tingle.

"Shucks!" exclaimed Jim-Polk, in a dis-
gusted tone. "It's old Loud, and we won't
hear from Jolly till the coon's track is hot
enough to raise a blister."

Again Loud opened, and again, and always
with increasing spirit, and his voice, borne over
the woods and fields on the night winds, was
most musical.

"Oh, my goodness!" cried Jim-Polk; "if I
had Jolly here, I'd kill him. No, I wouldn't,
neither!" he exclaimed, excitedly. "Just listen! he's a-puttin' in now!" With that he gave
a yell that fairly woke the echoes and caused
Mr. Snelson to jump.

"Upon me soul!" said that worthy gentleman, "ye'll never die wit' consumption. In me
books I've read of them that made the welkin
ring, but I've never heard it rung before."

"Shucks!" said Jim-Polk; "wait till Harbert there gets stirred up."

It was true that Jolly, as Jim-Polk expressed

it, had "put in." The scent was warm enough to cure his sulkiness. Running in harmony and giving mouth alternately, and sometimes together, the music the two dogs made was irresistibly inspiring, and when Harbert at intervals lifted up his voice to cheer them on even Mr. Snelson glowed with excitement and enthusiasm.

"Now, then, Harbert," said Jim-Polk, "you can light your carriage-lamps, and by that time we'll know which way we've got to trot."

The torches were soon lit, one for Jim-Polk and one for Harbert, and then they paused to listen to the dogs.

"That coon has been caught out from home," said Jim-Polk, after a pause. "The dogs are between him and his hollow tree. He's makin' for that dreen in pap's ten-acre field. There's a pond there, and old Zip has gone there after a bait of frogs. Just wait till they turn his head this way."

"Tut, tut, young man!" exclaimed Mr. Snelson, with something like a frown. "Ye talk like somebody readin' from a book—upon me word ye do—and if that was all I'd not disagree wit' ye; but ye go on and talk for all the world

like ye had yure two blessed eyes on the coon
all the time. Come! if ye know all that, how
d'ye know it?"

"Well, sir," said Jim-Polk, "the coon is
three quarters of an hour ahead of the dogs—
maybe a little more, maybe a little less. How
do I know it? Why, because I know my dogs.
They ain't on their mettle. They ain't runnin'
at more than half speed, if that. I can tell by
the way they open on the trail. Old Loud is
takin' his time. When he gets the coon started
home you'll hear him fairly lumber. How do
I know the coon is goin' away from home?
Shucks! My sev'n senses tell me that. We
started out early. So did old Zip. He was at
the pond huntin' for frogs when he heard old
Louder open. If he's struck out on t'other side
of the dreen we'll have to wait tell the dogs
fetch him back to the creek. If he struck out
on this side, he'll come right down the hollow below here. Let's see what the dogs
say."

"Deyer 'livenin' up," said Harbert.

The hunters walked a few hundred yards to
the verge of the slope that led to the bed of the
creek. Suddenly the dogs were silent. Ten

seconds — twenty ; a half-minute passed, and nothing could be heard of the dogs.

"We may as well return home," said Mr. Snelson. "The ravenous beasts have overtaken him, and they'll lay by till they've devoured him. Upon me soul, it's queer tastes they have !"

"Oh, no," replied Jim-Polk. "Dogs'll eat rabbits and squirrels, but they never eat coons nor 'possums. You'll hear from Jolly and Loud terreckly, and then they'll be a-gallantin' old Zip home. Just listen !"

As he spoke Loud gave mouth with a roar that filled the woods, and he was immediately joined by Jolly, whose quicker and more decisive voice chimed in as a pleasant accompaniment.

"They are comin' right this way !" exclaimed Jim-Polk, breathlessly. "Don't make a fuss— just be right still, so's not to skeer the coon across the creek. Jewhillikens ! Jest listen at old Loud a-lumberin' !"

And it was worth listening to. The mettle of the dog—of both dogs—was now fairly up, and they gave voice with a heat and vigor that could hardly have been improved upon if they had been in sight of the fleeing raccoon. They seemed to be running at full speed. They passed within twenty yards of where the hunters stood, snorting fiercely as they caught their breath to bark. As they went by, Harbert sent a wild halloo after them that seemed to add to their ardor.

"Now, then," exclaimed Jim-Polk, "we've got to go. You take the axe, Harbert, and let Joe take your light."

Raising his torch aloft, Jim-Polk sprang forward after the dogs, closely followed by Joe Maxwell and Harbert, while Mr. Snelson brought up the rear. The clever printer was not a woodsman, and he made his way through the undergrowth and among the trees with great difficulty. Once, when he paused for a moment to disentangle his legs from the embrace of a bamboo brier, he found himself left far in the rear, and he yelled lustily to his companions.

"Mother of Moses!" he exclaimed at the top of his voice, "will ye be after leavin' me in the wilderness?"

But for the quick ear of Harbert, he would assuredly have been left. The other hunters waited for him, and he came up puffing and blowing.

"I could cut a cord o' wood wit' half the exertion!" he exclaimed. "Come, boys! let's sit down an' have an understandin'. Me legs and me whole body politic have begun for to cry out agin this harum-scarum performance. Shall we go slower, or shall ye pick me up an' carry me?"

The boys were willing to compromise, but in the ardor of the chase they would have forgotten Mr. Snelson if that worthy gentleman had not made his presence known by yelling at them whenever they got too far ahead. The dogs ran straight down the creek for a mile at full speed. Suddenly Jim-Polk cried out:

"They've treed!"

"Yasser!" said Harbert, with a loud whoop; "dey mos' sholy is!"

"Then," said Mr. Snelson, sarcastically, "the fun is all over—the jig is up. 'Tis a thousand pities."

"Not much!" exclaimed Jim-Polk. "The fun's just begun. A coon ain't kotch jest because he's up a tree."

"Well, sir," said Mr. Snelson, with a serious

air, "if they've got wings, upon me soul, we should have fetched a balloon."

When the hounds were trailing there was a mellow cadence in their tones which was not to be heard when they barked at the tree. They gave mouth more deliberately, and in a measured way.

When the hunters arrived the hounds were alternately baying and gnawing at the foot of the tree.

" Bark to bark!" exclaimed Mr. Snelson, with much solemnity. His little joke was lost on all save Joe Maxwell, who was too much interested in the coon to laugh at it.

Much to Harbert's delight, the tree was not a large one, and he made immediate preparations to cut it down.

" Wait a minit," said Jim-Polk. " This coon ain't at home, and we'd better be certain of the tree he is in."

" You must have been visitin' him," said the genial printer, " for how de ye know about his home, else?"

" Some of these days," said Jim-Polk, laughing, " I'll come to your house an' stay to dinner, an' tell you about how coons live in holler trees."

"Fetch your dinner wit' ye," responded Snelson, "and ye're more than welcome."

Jim-Polk was too busy to make a reply. Holding the torch behind him, and waving it slowly, he walked around the tree. He appeared to be investigating his own shadow, which flickered and danced in the leaves and branches. Now stooping and peering, now tip-toeing and craning his neck, now leaning to the right and now to the left, he looked into the top of the tree. Finally, he exclaimed :

"Here he is, Joe! Come, take a look at him."

Joe tried his best to see the coon. He looked where Jim-Polk pointed, taking sight along his finger, but he was obliged to confess that he could see nothing

"Gracious alive!" cried Jim-Polk, "can't you see his eyes a-shinin' in the leaves there?"

"Pshaw!" exclaimed Joe; "I was looking for the whole coon, and I thought the shiny things were stars showing between the leaves."

But no stars ever burned as steadily as the pale-green little orbs that shone in the tree.

"Maybe," said Mr. Snelson, after trying in vain to "shine" the coon's eyes—"maybe the

creature has left his eyes there and escaped."
But the others paid no attention to his jocu-
larity.

"The thing to do now, Harbert," said Jim-
Polk, "is to lay that tree where it won't hit up
agin no other tree, because if we don't we'll
have to be a-cuttin' an' a-slashin' in here all
night."

"So!" exclaimed Mr. Snelson, in a tragic
tone. "Well, then, I'll der-raw the der-rapery
of me couch about me and lie down to pleasant
der-reams!'"

"You see," said Jim-Polk, "if that tree hits
agin another tree, off goes Mr. Zip Coon into
t'other one. Coon is quicker'n lightnin' on the
jump."

"I'll make 'er fall out dat way." Harbert
indicated an open place by a wave of his hand.

"Upon me soul!" exclaimed Mr. Snelson,
"I didn't know you could make a tree fall up
hill."

"Yes, suh!".said Harbert, with pardonable
pride. "I done cleaned out too many new
groun's. I lay I kin drive a stob out dar an'
put de body er dish yer tree right 'pon top un
it. I kin dat!"

With that Harbert rolled up his sleeves, displaying the billowy muscles of his arms, wiped the blade of the axe, spat in his hands, swung the axe around his head, and buried it deep in the body of the water-oak. It was a sweeping, downward stroke, and it was followed quickly by others until in a very short time the tree began to sway a little. The dogs, which had ceased their baying, now became restless and ran wildly about, but always keeping a safe distance from the tree. Mr. Snelson took his stand on one side and Joe Maxwell on the other, while Jim-Polk went out where the tree was to fall, after cautioning Harbert to keep a lookout for the coon. The advice to Harbert was given with good reason, for it is a favorite trick of the raccoon to start down the body of the tree as it falls and leap off while the dogs and hunters are looking for him in the bushy top.

This coon made the same experiment. As the tree swayed forward and fell, he ran down the trunk. Mr. Snelson saw him, gave a squall, and rushed forward to grab him. At the same moment Harbert gave a yell that was a signal to the dogs, and the excited creatures plunged toward him. Whether it was Jolly or whether it was Loud, no one ever knew, but one of the dogs, in his excitement, ran between Mr. Snelson's legs. That gentleman's heels flew in the air, and he fell on his back with a resounding thump. Stunned and frightened, he hardly knew what had happened. The last thing he saw was the coon, and he concluded that he had captured the animal.

"Murder!" he screamed. "Run here an' take 'em off! Run here! I've got 'em!"

Then began a terrific struggle between Mr. Snelson and a limb of the tree that just touched his face, and this he kept up until he was lifted to his feet. He made a ridiculous spectacle as he stood there glaring angrily around as if trying to find the man or the animal that had knocked him down and pummeled him. His coat was ripped and torn, and his pantaloons were split at both knees. He seemed to realize the figure he cut in the eyes of his companions.

"Oh, laugh away!" he cried. "'Tis yure opportunity. The next time it will be at some one else ye're laughing. Upon me soul!" he went on, examining himself, "I'd ha' fared

better in the battle of Manassus. So this is
your coon-hunting, is it? If the Lord and the
coon'll forgive me for me share in this night's
worruk, the devil a coon will I hunt any more
whatever."

Meanwhile the coon had jumped from the
tree, with the hounds close behind him. They
had overrun him on the hill, and this gave him
an opportunity to get back to the swamp, where
the dogs could not follow so rapidly. Yet the
coon had very little the advantage. As Jim-
Polk expressed it, "the dogs had their teeth on
edge," and they were rushing after him without
any regard for brake or brier, lagoon or quag-
mire. The only trouble was with Mr. Snelson,
who declared that he was fagged out.

"Well," says Jim-Polk, "we've got to keep
in hearin' of the dogs. The best we can do is
to fix you up with a light an' let you follow
along the best way you can. You couldn't get
lost if you wanted to, 'cause all you've got to do
is to follow the creek, an' you're boun' to ketch
up with us."

So Mr. Snelson, in spite of his prediction that
he would get lost in the wilderness, and be devoured by the wild beasts, to say nothing of

being frightened to death by owls, was provided
with a torch.   Then the boys and Harbert
made a dash in the direction of the dogs.   If
they thought to leave Mr. Snelson, they reck-
oned ill, for that worthy man, flourishing the
torch over his head, managed to keep them in
sight.

"The dogs are not very far away," said Joe.
"They ought to have gone a couple of miles by
this time."

"Old Zip is in trouble," said Jim-Polk.   "He
has been turnin' an' doublin', an' twistin', an'
squirmin'.   He can't shake ole Loud off, an' he
can't git home.   So what's he goin' to do?"

"Climb another tree, I reckon," said Joe.

"Not much!" exclaimed Jim.   "He'll take
to water."

The dogs got no farther away, but the chase
still kept up.   The coon seemed to be going in
all directions, across and around, and presently
the dogs began to bay.

"He's gone in a-washin'!" exclaimed Jim-
Polk, with a yell.

"Bless me soul! and how do ye know that?"
exclaimed Mr. Snelson, who came up puffing
and blowing.

"Oh, I know mor'n that," said Jim-Polk. "The coon's in the water, 'cause when the dogs bark at him it don't soun' like it did when they had their heads in the air; an' he's in swimmin' water, 'cause, if he wan't, he'd a' been kilt by this time."

It was as Jim-Polk said. When the hunters reached the dogs they could see the coon swimming around and around in the center of a small lagoon, while the dogs were rushing about on the banks.

"I wish to goodness," exclaimed Harbert, "dat dey wuz some young dogs wid us, bekaze den we'd have de biggest kind er fight. Dey'd swim in dar atter dat coon, an' he'd fetch um a swipe er two, an' den jump on der heads an' duck um. Gentermens! he sholy is a big un."

"You're right!" exclaimed Jim-Polk. "He's one of the old-timers. He'd put up a tremenjus fight if he didn't have old Loud to tackle. —Fetch him out, boys!" he cried to the dogs, "fetch him out!"

Long experience had taught the dogs their tactics. Jolly swam in and engaged the coon's attention, while Loud followed, swimming sidewise toward the center. Jolly swam around slowly, while Loud seemed to drift toward the coon, still presenting a broadside, so to speak. The coon, following the movements of Jolly, had paid no attention to Loud. Suddenly he saw the dog, and sprang at him, but it was too late. Loud ducked his head, and, before the coon could recover, fastened his powerful jaws on the creature's ribs. There was a loud squall, a fierce shake, and the battle was over.

But before the dog could bring the coon to the bank, Mr. Snelson uttered a paralyzing shriek and ran for the water. Harbert tried to hold him back.

"Ouch! loose me! loose me! I'll brain ye if ye don't loose me!"

Shaking Harbert off, the printer ran to the edge of the lagoon, and soused his hand and arm in the water. In his excitement he had held the torch straight over his head, and the hot pitch from the fat pine had run on his hand and down his sleeve.

"Look at me!" he exclaimed, as they went slowly homeward. "Just look at me! The poor wife'll have to doctor me body an' darn me clothes, an' they're all I've got to me name.

If ye'll stand by me, Joe," he went on patheti-
cally, " I'll do your worruk meself, but ye shall
have two afternoons next week." And Joe
Maxwell " stood by " Mr. Snelson the best he
could.

CHAPTER VIII.

SOMETHING ABOUT "SANDY CLAUS."

HARBERT'S house on the Turner place was not far from the kitchen, and the kitchen itself was only a few feet removed from the big house; in fact, there was a covered passageway between them. From the back steps of the kitchen two pieces of hewn timber, half buried in the soil, led to Harbert's steps, thus forming, as the negro called it, a wet-weather path, over which Mr. Turner's children could run when the rest of the yard had been made muddy by the fall and winter rains.

Harbert's house had two rooms and two fireplaces. One of the rooms was set apart for him and his wife, while the other was used as a weaving-room. In one Harbert used to sit at night and amuse the children with his reminiscences and his stories; in the other Aunt Crissy used to weave all day and sing, keeping time with the flying shuttle and the dancing slays. The children might tire of their toys, their ponies, and everything else, but they could always find something to interest them in Harbert's house. There were few nights, especially during the winter, that did not find them seated by the negro's white hearthstone. On special occasions they could hardly wait to finish supper before going out to see him. Sometimes they found Aunt Crissy there, and as she was fat and good-humored—not to say jolly—she was always a welcome guest, so far as the children were concerned. As for Harbert, it was all one to him whether Aunt Crissy was present or not. To use his own sententious phrase, she was welcome to come or she was welcome to stay away. Frequently Joe Maxwell would go and sit there with them, especially when he was feeling lonely and homesick.

One evening, in the early part of December, the children hurried through their supper of bread and butter and milk, and ran to Harbert's house. Aunt Crissy was there, and her fat face and white teeth shone in the firelight as she sat smiling at the youngsters.

"I done got Chris'mas in my bones," she was saying, as Wattie and Willie entered.

"Well, I ain't gwine ter say dat," said Harbert, "kaze I'm dat ole dat I ain't got no roomance in my bones fer nothin' 'tall, 'ceppin' 'tis de rheumatism; yit dat don't hender Chris'mas, an' I ain't makin' no deniance but what hit's in de a'r."

"Now you er talkin'," exclaimed Aunt Crissy, with unction. "You mos' sholy is."

There was a little pause, and then Harbert cried out:

"In de name er goodness, des lissen at dat!"

What was it? The wind, rising and falling, ebbing and flowing like the great waves of the sea, whistled under the eaves, and sighed mournfully over the chimney. But it was not the wind that Harbert heard. There was a sharp rattling on the shingles and a swift pattering at the windows. Harbert and Aunt Crissy looked at each other and then at the children.

"What is it?" asked Wattie, drawing a little closer to Harbert.

"Pshaw! I know what it is," said Willie, "it's sleet." Harbert shook his head gravely as he gazed in the fire.

"It mought be," he said, "an' den agin it moughtn't. It mought be ole Sandy Claus sorter skirmishin' roun' an' feelin' his way."

"Trufe, too," said Aunt Crissy, falling in with the idea. "He moughtn't want to skeer nobody, so he des let folks b'lieve tain't nothin' but sleet. Dey tells me dat ole man Sandy Claus is monstus slick."

"He bleedze ter be slick," remarked Harbert, "kaze I bin livin' yere, off an' on, a mighty long time, an' I ain't saw 'im yit. An' I let you know hit got ter be a mighty slick man dat kin dodge me all dis time. He got to be bofe slick an' peart."

"Yasser," said Aunt Crissy, holding her apron up by the corner, and looking at it thoughtfully; "he slick fer true. He light 'pon top er de house same ez a jay-bird, an' dey ain't no scufflin' when he slide down de chimberly."

"Dey sez," said Harbert, in a reminiscent way—"dey sez dat he rubs hisse'f wid goose-grease fer ter make he j'ints limber an' loose; when he got dis yere grease on 'im dey can't nobody ketch 'im, kaze he'd slip right out'n der han's."

" I speck dat's so," said Aunt Crissy, " kaze one time when I wuz livin' wid Marse Willyum Henry an' sleepin' in de house in time er Chris'-mas, I tuck'n he'p'd de chillun hang up der stockin's. After dey all got ter bed, I sot by de fier a-noddin'. How long I sot dar I'll never tell you, but all of a sudden I yeard a turrible racket. I gun a jump, I did, an' open my eyes. De outside do' wuz open, an' stannin' dar wuz one er Marse Willyum Henry's houn' dogs. He stood dar, he did, wid his bristles up, an' dar in de middle er the flo' wuz de ole cat. Her back wuz all bowed up, an' her tail "—here Aunt Crissy paused and looked all around the room as if in search of something with which to com-pare the old cat's tail—" I ain't tellin' you no lie ; dat cat tail wuz bigger 'roun' dan my arm ! "

" I don't 'spute it," exclaimed Harbert, with fervor, " dat I don't."

" An' dat ain't all." Aunt Crissy closed her eyes and threw her head back, as if to add em-phasis to what she was about to say. " Dat ain't all—dem ar stockin's wuz done fulled up wid goodies, an' dey wuz done fulled up whilst I wuz a-settin' right dar." No style of type has yet been invented that would convey even a

faint idea of the impressive tone in which Aunt
Cissy made this startling announcement.

"Ole Sandy wuz gittin' you in close quarters, mon," exclaimed Harbert.

"Man, you er talkin' now," said Aunt
Crissy. "I wuz settin' right spang at de fier-
place," she went on, describing her position
with appropriate gestures, "an' I could er des
retched out my han'—so—an' totched de stockin's, an' yit, 'spite er dat, 'long come ole Sandy
Claus, whilst I wuz settin' dar noddin' an' fulled
um up. Dat des what he done. He come, he
did, an' fulled um up right fo' my face. Ef my
eyes had er des bin open I'd a seed 'im, an' ef
I'd a seed 'im, I'd a grabbed 'im right by de
coat-tail. Yasser! I'd a grabbed 'im ef he'd a
kyar'd me up de chimberly."

Wattie and Willie listened open-mouthed,
so intense was their interest; and so, it may
be said, did Joe Maxwell. But now Willie
spoke:

"Suppose you had caught him, Aunt Crissy,
what would you have done then?"

"Shoo, honey! I'd a helt him hard an' fas':
I'd a rastled wid 'im, an' when he 'gun ter git
de better un me, I'd a squalled out same ez one

er dez yere wil' cats. I'd a squalled so loud I'd
a fair 'larmed de settlement."

Aunt Crissy paused, folded her fat arms
across her broad bosom and looked in the fire.
Harbert, with a long pair of tongs, as musical as
those that Shakespeare wrote about, put the
noses of the chunks together, and carefully
placed a fat pine knot in the center. Then he
leaned back in his chair, and rubbed his chin
thoughtfully.

"Well," said he, after a while, "I dunno ez
I bin close to ole Sandy Claus as what you is,
Sis Crissy, but I bin mighty close, an' 'tain't bin
so mighty long ago needer. One night des 'fo'
Chris'mas I wuz gwine 'long thoo de woods
close by de Ward place. I wuz gwine 'long, I
wuz, sorter studyin' wid myse'f 'bout whedder I
ought ter hang up my stockin's wid de res' er
de folks, when, fus news I know, look like I kin
year de win' blowin'. Hit soun' so loud dat I
stop right in my tracks an ax myse'f what de
name er goodness is de matter. I ain't feel no
win' an' I ain't see no bush shakin', but up dar
in de top er de trees hit look like dey wuz a
reg'lar hurrycane a blowin'. Man, sir! she fair
roared up dar, yit I ain't see no win', an' I ain't

see no bush a shakin'. Hit make me feel so
quare dat ef a hick'y-nut had a drapped any-
whar nigh me, I'd a broke an' run fum dar
like de Ole Boy wuz atter me. Hit make me
feel so funny dat I ain't know whedder it wuz
ole man Harbert out dar, or some yuther nigger
dat done got los' in some new country. I stood
dar, I did, en des waited fer sump'n ner ter happen, but bimeby de noise all quit, an' de roarin'
died down, twel you could a yeard a pin drop.
I kotch my bref, I did, an' I 'low ter myself
dat all dat racket up in de a'r dar mus' sholy
a-bin ole Sandy Claus agwine sailin' by. Dat
what I had in my min', yit I ain't stop dar fer
ter make no inquirements. I des put out, I did,
an' I went a polin' home, an' it make me feel
mighty good when I got dar."

The children visited Harbert's house every
night for several nights before Christmas, but
somehow they didn't seem to enjoy themselves.
Harbert was so busy with one thing and another
that they felt themselves in the way. They had
the ardor and the hope of childhood, however, and
they continued their visits with persistent regularity. They were very patient, comparatively
speaking, and their patience was finally rewarded.

The night before Christmas, when their interests and expectations were on the point of culmination, they found Harbert sitting in front of the fire, his head thrown back and his hands folded in his lap; and before the little ones could fix themselves comfortably, Aunt Crissy walked in and flung herself into a chair.

"*Whoo-ee!*" she exclaimed. "I'm dat tired dat I can't skacely drag one foot 'fo' de yuther. Look like I bin on my feet mighty nigh a mont', dat it do, an' I'm dat stiff, I feel like some er my lim's gwine ter break in two. Dey ain't nothin' on dis plantation dat I ain't had my han's in, 'specially ef it's work. It's Crissy yere, an Crissy dar, de whole blessed time, an' I dun' ner what de lazy niggers 'roun' yere would do ef Crissy wuz to take a notion ter peg out. Mistiss got old Charity in de kitchin' dar a-cookin' an' a-growlin', but when dey's any nice cookin' ter be done, Crissy got ter go an' do it. I wouldn't mind it so much," Aunt Crissy went on, "ef dem yuther niggers'd do like dey tuck some intruss in what's gwine on, but you know yo'se'f, Brer Harbert, how no 'count dey is."

"Ah, Lord! you nee'nt ter tell me, Sis

Crissy, I know um; I know um all. An' yit dey'll all be scrougin' one ane'r 'fo' day arter termorrow mornin' fer ter see which gwine ter be de fus fer ter holler Chris'mas gif' at marster an' mistiss. Now you watch um! dey'll all be dar, an' dey ain't none un um skacely yearned der salt. I'm mighty nigh run down. Dis mornin' de stock in de lot wuz a hollerin' fer der feed, an' it wuz broad daylight at dat. Den dar wuz de milkin': hit wuz atter sun-up 'fo' dat Marthy Ann got ter de cow-pen. Dat gal blood kin ter you, Sis Crissy, but I done laid de law down; I done tole 'er dat de nex' time she come creepin' out dat late, I wuz gwine to whirl in an' gi' 'er a frailin', an' I'm gwine to do it ef de Lord spar's me."

"Nummine 'bout no kinnery, Brer Harbert," said Aunt Crissy, with emphasis. "You des git you a brush an' wa'r dat gal out. She new han' wid de cows, but tooby sho' she kin git out 'fo' sun-up."

"I'm mighty glad," Harbert remarked, glancing at the children, who were not at all interested in the "worriments" of those faithful negroes—"I'm mighty glad dat Chris'mas is so nigh. De corn done in de crib, de fodder in de barn, de cotton 'n de gin-house, de hogs done kilt an' put up, an' ef Charity ain't might'ly behindhand de turkey done in de pot. Dat bein' de case, what mo' kin we ax, 'ceptin' we git down yere on de flo' an' ax a blessin'?"

"Trufe, too!" exclaimed Aunt Crissy. "I ain't quollin', but dem niggers is so owdacious lazy dat dey keeps me pestered."

"Yasser!" continued Harbert, "de signs all look like deyer right. When I sets right flat down an' run it all over, hit make me feel so good dat I got a great mine fer ter hang up my sock right dar side er de chimbly-jam, an' set up yere an' watch fer ter see ole Sandy Claus come a-slidin' down. Ef his foot wuz ter slip, an' he wuz ter drap down on dat pot-rack dar, I lay he'd wake up de whole plantation. My sock ain't so mighty long in de leg," Harbert went on, reflectively, "but she mighty big in de foot, an' ef ole Sandy Claus wuz ter take a notion fer ter fill 'er plum up, she'd lighten his wallet might'ly."

"Did you ever hang up your stockings, Harbert?" asked Willie.

"Why, tooby sho', honey," replied the negro, laughing. "I bin hang um up way back yander 'fo' you wuz born'd. An' I used ter git goodies in um, too. Lord! dem wuz times, sho' nuff. I used ter git goodies in um dem days, but now I speck I wouldn't git so much ez a piece er 'lasses candy. But, nummine 'bout dat! I'll des take en hang um up dis night, an' I'll be mighty glad ef I git a slishe er cracklin' bread. Dat kinder bread good nuff for me, 'specially when it right fresh."

"Man, don't talk!" exclaimed Aunt Crissy. "Look like I kin in about tas'e it now!"

"Aunt Crissy, are you going to hang up your stockings?" asked Wattie.

"Bless yo' soul, honey! I mos' got in de notion un it. Ef 'twan't dat I'm a sleepin' up in old Granny Chaney house fer ter sorter keep 'er comp'ny, I speck I would hang um up. But dey tells me dat 'twon't do no good ef you hang up yo' stockin's in some un else house. 'Sides dat, ole Granny Chaney so restless dat she'd in about skeer old Sandy Claus off ef he 'uz to start ter come. I'm a tellin' you de trufe, Brer Harbert, dat ole creetur done got so dat she don't skacely close 'er eyes fer sleep de whole blessed night. She take so many naps endurin' 'er de day, dat when night come she des ez wakeful ez dat ole black cat what stay up dar at de barn."

"Dat ole 'oman gittin' ole, mon," said Harbert. "She wuz done grown an' had chillun when I wuz little baby. She lots older dan what I is, an' I ain't no chicken myse'f. I speck ef she 'uz ter go back an' count up 'er Chris'mases, she done seed mighty nigh ez many ez what ole Sandy Claus is."

"Well," said Aunt Crissy, changing the subject, "I ain't gwine hang up no stockin', kaze I speck dat whatsomever ole Sandy Claus got fer me, he'll drap it som'rs in de big house, an' when I holler at marster an' mistiss in de mornin', dey'll fetch it out."

"Dat's so," said Harbert. "Yit I got a mighty good notion fer ter hang up mine an' take de resk. But I'd a heap ruther git sumpin' dat's too big fer ter go in um."

"Well, we are going to hang up our stockings," said Willie. "I'm going to hang up both of mine, and Wattie says she's going to hang up both of hers."

"Dat's right, honey; an' if dat ain't 'nuff' whirl in an' hang up a meal-sack. I done bin year tell 'fo' now 'bout folks what hang up great big bags stidder der stockin's. Whedder dey got any mo' dan t'er folks is mo' dan I kin tell you."

"Harbert," said Wattie, "do you reckon we'll git anything at all?"

"Oh, I speck so," said the negro. "I ain't year talk er you bein' so mighty bad dis long time. You cuts up scan'lous sometimes, but it's kaze yo' buddy dar pesters you."

This suggestion made Willie so angry that he threatened to go back to the big house and go to bed, and he would have gone but for a remark made by Aunt Crissy—a remark that made him forget his anger.

"Dey tells me," said Aunt Crissy, in a sub- dued tone, "dat de cows know when Chris'mas come, an' many's de time I year my mammy say dat when twelve o'clock come on Chris'mas- eve night, de cows gits down on der knees in de lot an' stays dat-away some little time. Ef any- body else had er tole me dat I'd a des hooted at um, but, mammy, she say she done seed um do it. I ain't never seed um do it myse'f, but mammy say she seed um."

"I bin year talk er dat myse'f," said Harbert, reverently, "an' dey tells me dat de cattle gits down an' prays bekaze dat's de time when de Lord an' Saviour wuz born'd."

"Now, don't dat beat all!" exclaimed Aunt Crissy. "Ef de dumb creeturs kin say der pra'rs, I dunner what folks ought ter be doin'."

"An' dar's de chickens," Harbert went on— "look like dey know der's sump'n up. Dis ve'y night I year de roosters crowin' fo' sev'n o'clock. I year tell dat dey crows so soon in sign dat Peter made deniance un his Lord an' Marster."

"I speck dat's so," said Aunt Crissy.

"Hit bleedze ter be so," responded the old man with the emphasis that comes from con-viction.

Then he intimated that it was time for the children to go to bed if they wanted to get up early the next morning to see what Sandy Claus had brought. This was a suggestion the young-sters could appreciate, and they scrambled out of the door and went racing to the big house.

Before sunrise the plantation was in a stir. The negroes, rigged out in their Sunday clothes, were laughing, singing, wrestling, and playing. The mules and horses having been fed and turned in the pasture for a holiday, were caper-ing about; the cows were lowing in a satisfied manner, the dogs were barking, the geese screaming, the turkeys "yelping" and gobbling, and the chickens cackling. A venerable billy-goat, with a patriarchal beard and the rings of many summers marked on his broad and crumpled horns, had marched up one of the long arms of the packing-screw and was now perched motionless on the very pinnacle of that quaint structure, making a picturesque addition to the landscape, as he stood outlined against the reddening eastern sky.

Willie and Wattie were up so early that they had to feel for their stockings in the dark, and their exclamations of delight, when they found them well filled, aroused the rest of the household. By the time breakfast was over the negroes were all assembled in the yard, and they seemed to be as happy as the children, as their laughter and their antics testified. Towering above them all was Big Sam, a giant in size and a child in disposition. He was noted for miles around for his feats of strength. He could shoulder a bale of cotton weighing five hundred pounds, and place it on a wagon; and though he was proud of his ability in this direction, he was not too proud to be the leader in all the frolics. He was even fuller of laughter and good-humor than his comrades, and on this particular morning, while the negroes were waiting for the usual Christmas developments, Big Sam, his eyes glistening and his white teeth shining, struck up the melody of a plantation play-song, and in a few minutes the dusky crowd had arranged itself in groups, each and all joining in the song. No musical director ever had a more melodious chorus than that which followed the leadership of Big Sam. It was not a trained chorus, to be sure, but the melody that it gave to the winds of the morning was freighted with a quality indescribably touching and tender.

In the midst of the song Mr. Turner appeared on the back piazza, and instantly a shout went up:

"Chris'mas gif', marster! Chris'mas gif'!" and then, a moment later, there was a cry of "Chris'mas gif', mistiss!"

"Where is Harbert?" inquired Mr. Turner, waving his hand and smiling.

"Here me, marster!" exclaimed Harbert, coming forward from one of the groups.

"Why, you haven't been playing, have you?"

"I bin tryin' my han', suh, an' I monst'us

glad you come out, kaze I ain't nimble like I useter wuz. Dey got me in de middle er dat ring dar, an' I couldn't git out nohow."

"Here are the store-room keys. Go and open the door, and I will be there directly."

It was a lively crowd that gathered around the wide door of the store-room. For each of the older ones there was a stiff dram apiece, and for all, both old and young, there was a present of some kind. The presents were of a substantial character, too. Those who had made crops of their own found a profitable market right at their master's door. Some of them had made as much as two bales of cotton on the land they were permitted to cultivate, while others had made good crops of corn—all of which was bought by their master.

Then the big six-mule wagon was brought into service, and into this was packed the horse-collars, made of shucks and wahoo-bark, the baskets, the foot-mats, the brooms, the walking-canes, and the axe-helves, that were to find a market in the town nine miles away.

In spite of the war, it was a happy time, and Joe Maxwell was as happy as any of the rest.

CHAPTER IX.

DESERTERS AND RUNAWAYS.

ALL was peace on the plantation, but war has long arms, and it dropped its gifts of poverty and privation in many a humble home with which Joe Maxwell was familiar. War has its bill of fare, too, and much of it was not to Joe's taste. For coffee there were various substitutes: sweet potatoes, chipped and dried, parched meal, parched rye, parched okra-seeds, and sassafras tea. Joe's beverage was water sweetened with sorghum-sirup, and he found it a very refreshing and wholesome drink. Some of the dishes that were popular in the old colonial days were revived. There was persimmon bread; what could be more toothsome than that? Yet a little of it went a long way, as Mr. Wall used to say. And there was potato pone—sweet potatoes boiled, kneaded, cut into pones, and baked. And then there was callalou—a mixture of collards, poke salad, and turnip greens boiled for dinner and fried over for supper. This was the invention of Jimsy, an old negro brought over from the West Indies,

Zimzi.

whose real name was Zimzi, and who always ran away when anybody scolded him.

The old-fashioned loom and spinning-wheel were kept going, and the women made their own dyes. The girls made their hats of rye and wheat straw, and some very pretty bonnets were made of the fibrous substance that grows in the vegetable known as the bonnet squash.

It was agreed on all sides that times were very hard, and yet they seemed very pleasant and comfortable to Joe Maxwell. He had never seen money more plentiful. Everybody seemed to have some, and yet nobody had enough. It was all in Confederate bills, and they were all new and fresh and crisp. Joe had some of it himself, and he thought he was growing rich. But the more plentiful the money became, the higher went the price of everything.

After a while Joe noticed that the older men became more serious. There were complaints in the newspapers of speculators and extortioners—of men who imposed on and mistreated the widows and wives of the soldiers. And then there was a law passed preventing the farmers from planting only so many acres of land in cotton, in order that more food might be raised for the army. After this came the impressment law, which gave the Confederate officials the right to seize private property, horses, mules, and provisions. And then came the conscription law.

There was discontent among the men who were at home, but they were not left to make any serious complaints. One by one the conscript officers seized all except those who were exempt and hurried them off to the front. Those who thought it a disgrace to be conscripted either volunteered or hired themselves as substitutes.

This is the summing up of the first three years of the war, so far as it affected Joe Maxwell. The impression made upon him was of slow and gradual growth. He only knew that trouble and confusion were abroad in the land. He could see afterward what a lonely and desperate period it must have been to those who had kinsmen in the war; but, at that time, all these things were as remote from him as a dream that is half remembered. He set up the editor's articles, criticising Governor Joe Brown for some attacks he had made on the Confederate Government, without understanding them fully; and he left Mr. Wall, the hatter, who was a violent secessionist, to discuss the situation with Mr. Bonner, the overseer, who was a Whig, and something of a Union man.

Late one afternoon, after listening to a heated

dispute between Mr. Wall and Mr. Bonner, Joe concluded that he would take a run in the fields with the harriers. So he called and whistled for them, but they failed to come. Harbert thought they had followed some of the plantation hands, but, as this rarely happened, Joe was of the opinion that they had gone hunting on their own account. They were very busy and restless little dogs, and it was not uncommon for them to go rabbit-hunting for themselves. Going toward Mr. Snelson's, Joe thought he could hear them running a rabbit on the farther side of the plantation. He went in that direction, but found, after a while, that they were running in the Jack Adams place, and as he went nearer they seemed to get farther away. Finally, when he did come up with the dogs, he found that they were not the harriers at all, but a lot of curs and "fices." And then—how it happened he was never able to explain—Joe suddenly discovered that he was lost.

Perhaps if the idea had never occurred to him he would never have been lost, but the thought flashed in his mind and stayed there. He stood still in his tracks and looked all around, but the idea that he was really lost confused him. He was not frightened—he was not even uneasy. But he knew he was lost. Everything was strange and confusing. Even the sun, which was preparing to go to bed, was in the wrong place. Joe laughed at himself. Certainly he could return the way he came, so he faced about, as he thought, and started home.

Walking and running he went forward rapidly, and he had need to, for the sun had gone behind a cloud, and the cloud, black and threatening, was rising and filling the sky. How long he had been going Joe did not know, but suddenly he found himself near an old cabin. It was built of logs, and the chimney, which had been made of sticks and red clay, had nearly fallen down. The lad knew that this cabin was neither on the Turner plantation nor on the Jack Adams place. He had never heard any of the negroes allude to it, and he realized the fact that he had been running away from home.

Near the deserted house were the remnants of an orchard. A pear-tree, jagged and unshapely, grew not far from the door, while an apple-tree, with a part of its trunk rotted away, stood near a corner of the cabin. A growth of pines and scrub-oak showed that the place had been deserted for many a long year. A quarter of a mile away, through the gathering darkness, Joe could see a white fringe gleaming against the horizon. He knew that this was a fog, and that it rose from the river. Following the line of the fog, he could see that the cabin was in a bend of the river—the Horseshoe, as he had heard it called—and he knew that he was at least four miles from home. By this time the cloud had covered all the heavens. Away off in the woods he could hear the storm coming, sounding like a long-drawn sigh at first, and then falling with a sweeping rush and roar. Joe had no choice but to seek shelter in the old house. He was a stout-hearted youngster, and yet he could not resist the feeling of uneasiness and dread that came over him at the thought of spending the night in that lonely place. But there was no help for it. He could never find his way home in the darkness, and so he made the best of what seemed to him a very bad matter. The cabin was almost a wreck, but it served to keep off the rain.

Joe went in and explored the inside as care-

fully as he could in the darkness.   A wood-rat
or flying-squirrel rattled along the rafters as
he entered, and the loose puncheons of which
the floor was made bumped up and down as he
walked across them.   In one corner, as he went
groping about, he found a pile of shucks—corn-
husks—and straw, and he judged that the old
cabin had sometimes been used as a temporary
barn.   After satisfying himself that no other
person or creature had taken shelter there, Joe
tried to close the door.   He found this to be
a difficult matter.   The sill of the house had
settled so that the door was on the floor.   He
pushed it as far as it would go, and then groped
his way back to the shucks and quickly made
a bed of them.   He was fagged out, and the
shucks and straw made a comfortable pallet—so
comfortable, indeed, that by the time he had
made up his mind that it was a pleasant thing
to lie there and listen to the rain rushing down
on the weather-beaten roof, he was fast asleep.

How long he slept he did not know, but suddenly he awoke to discover that he was not the
only person who had sought shelter in the cabin.
The rain was still falling on the roof, but he
could hear some one talking in a low tone.   He

lay quite still and listened with all his ears. He soon discovered that the new-comers were negroes, whether two or three he could not tell. Presently he could distinguish what they said. The storm had ceased so that it no longer drowned their voices.

"I tell you what, mon," said one, "ole Injun Bill kin run ef he is chunky."

"Lor'! I had ter run ef I gwine fer keep up wid old Mink." said the other.

"Bless you!" responded the first voice, "I kin run when I git de invertation, else ole Bill Locke an' his nigger dogs would a done cotch me long ago."

"Dey ain't been atter me," said the second voice, "but I'm a spectin' un um eve'y day, an' when dey does—gentermen! I'm a-gwine ter scratch gravel! You hear what I tell you!"

"I come so fas'," remarked the first voice, "dat all dem ar buckeyes what I had done bounce outer my pocket."

"What you gwine fer do wid so many buck-eyes?" asked the second voice.

"Who? Me! Oh, I wuz des savin' um up fer dat ar white boy what stay 'long wid de print-in' machine," said the first voice. "He holp me

'long one time.   Harbert, he say dat white boy
is des ez good ter niggers ez ef dey all b'long
ter im, an' he say he got a head on 'im.   Dat
what Harbert say."

"I bin see 'im," said the second voice.   "I
don't like white folks myse'f, but I speck dat
boy got good in 'im.   He come fum town."

Joe Maxwell knew at once that one of the
voices belonged to Mink, the runaway, and he
judged that the other belonged to Injun Bill,
whose reputation was very bad.   He knew also
that the two negroes were talking about him,
and he was not only gratified at the compli-
ments paid him, but felt safer than if he had
been alone in the cabin.   In a spirit of mischief
he called out in a sepulchral tone of voice:

"Where's Mink?   I want Mink!"

He tried to imitate the tone that he had
heard mothers sometimes employ when they
are trying to frighten crying children into
silence with the bogie man.   There was no
reply from Mink, but Joe could hear the two
negroes breathing hard.   Then, imitating the
voice of a woman, he cried out:

"Where's Injun Bill?   I want Injun Bill!"

Imagining how horrified the negroes were,

and how they looked as they sat on the floor
quaking with terror, Joe could not restrain
himself.   He fell into a fit of uncontrollable
laughter that caused him to scatter the shucks
all over the floor.   This proceeding, wholly un-

Injun Bill, whose reputation was very bad.

accountable, added to the terror of the negroes.
Injun Bill, as it afterward appeared, made a
wild leap for the door, but his foot caught in a
crack in the floor and he fell headlong.   On top

of him fell Mink, and each thought he had been caught by the thing that had frightened him. They had a terrific scuffle on the floor, writhing over and under each other in their efforts to escape. Finally, Mink, who was the more powerful of the two, pinned Injun Bill to the floor.

"Who dis?" he cried, breathing hard with fear and excitement.

"Me! Dat who 'tis!" said Injun Bill, angrily. "What you doin' 'pon top er me?"

This complication caused Joe Maxwell to laugh until he could scarcely catch his breath. But at last he managed to control his voice.

"What in the name of goodness are you two trying to do?"

"Name er de Lord!" exclaimed Mink, "who is you, anyhow?"

"Dat what I like ter know," said Injun Bill, in a surly tone.

"Why, you've just been talking about me," replied Joe. "I lay there on the shucks and heard you give me a great name."

"Is dat you, little marster?" cried Mink. "Well, suh! Ef dat don't beat my time! How come you sech a fur ways fum yo' surroundin's?"

Joe explained as briefly as possible that he was lost.

"Well, well, well!" said Mink, by way of comment. "You sholy gimme a turn dat time. Little mo' an' I'd a thought de ole boy had me. Ef I'd a bin by myse'f when I hear dat callin' I lay I'd 'a to' down de whole side er de house. Dish yer nigger 'long wid me, little marster, he name Injun Bill. He say—"

"'Sh—sh!" said Injun Bill, softly. Then in a whisper—"watch out!"

Joe was about to say something, but suddenly he heard the sound of approaching footsteps. The negroes by a noiseless movement stepped close against the wall. Joe lay still. The new-comers entered the door without hesitation. They had evidently been there before.

"I'll take an' put my gun in the corner here," said one. "Now, don't go blunderin' aroun' an' knock it over; it might go off."

"All right," said the other. "Where is it? I'll put mine by it."

Then they seemed to be unfastening their belts.

"Hain't you got a match?" said one. "I'm

as wet as a drownded rat. I've got some kindlin' somewheres about my cloze. My will, ef I had it fried," he went on, " would be to be set down in front of a great big fireplace adryin' myse'f, an' a knowin' all the time that a great big tray of hot biscuit an' 'leven pounds of butter was a waitin' for me in the kitchen."

" Thunderation!" exclaimed the other, " don't talk that way. You make me so nervous I can't find the matches."

" Oh, well," said the first, " I was jist a thinkin' about eatin'. I wish Mink 'ud come on ef he's a-comin'."

" I done come, Mars John," said Mink.

" Confound your black hide!" exclaimed the man; " if I had my gun I'd shoot a hole spang throo you! Whadder you want to skeer me outn a year's growth for? If you're here, whyn't you sesso befo' you spoke?"

" Kaze I got comp'ny," said Mink.

The man gave a long whistle, denoting surprise. " Who've you got?" he asked, almost savagely.

" Injun Bill."

" Who else?"

" A white boy."

"Well, the great snakes! What sort of game is you up to? Who is the white boy?"

"He stay on the Turner plantation at de printin'-office," explained Mink.

"You hear that, don't you?" said the man to his companion. "And now it'll all be in the paper."

"Bosh!" exclaimed Joe. "I don't know you from a side of sole-leather. I got lost while rabbit-hunting, and came in here out of the rain."

"He's a peart-talkin' chap," said the man who wanted to eat a trayful of hot biscuits and eleven pounds of butter.

"He came fum town," said Mink, by way of explaining Joe's "peartness."

"How long since?" asked one of the men.

"Two years ago," said Joe.

After a little, one of the men succeeded in finding a match, and making a light with the pine kindlings that one of the two had brought. In a corner Mink found some pieces of dry wood and the small company soon had a fire burning. The weather was not cold, but the fire must have been very agreeable to the white men, who, as one of them expressed it, was "wringin' wet." These men took advantage of the first opportunity to examine Joe Maxwell very closely. They had evidently expected to find a much more formidable-looking person than he appeared to be, for one of them remarked to the other:

"Why, he hain't bigger'n a pound er soap arter a hard day's washin'."

"Naw!" said the other. "I've saw 'im befo'. He's that little rooster that useter be runnin' roun' town gittin' in all sorts er devilment. I reckon he's sorter out er his element here in the country."

"I've seen you, too," said Joe. "I've seen both of you. I used to see you drilling in the Hillsborough Rifles. I was at the depot when the company went off to the war."

The two men looked at each other in a peculiar way, and busied themselves trying to dry their clothes by the fire, standing close to the flickering flames. They were not handsome men, and yet they were not ill looking. One was short and stout, with black hair. He had a scar under one of his eyes that did not improve his appearance. But the expression of his face was pleasant in spite of this defect. The other was thin, tall, and stoop-shouldered. His beard was scanty and red, and his upper teeth protruded to such an extent that when his face was in repose they were exposed to view. But there was a humorous twinkle in his eyes that found an echo in his talk. Both men were growing gray. The dark man was Jim Wimberly, the other John Pruitt, and both had evidently seen hard times. Soldier-fashion, they made seats for themselves by sticking the ends of loose boards through the cracks, and allowing the other ends to rest on the floor. Thus they could sit or lie at full length as they chose. Joe fixed a seat for himself in the same way, while Mink and Injun Bill sat on the floor on each side of the fireplace.

"What do you call those here fellers," asked Mr. Pruitt, lighting his pipe with a splinter, and turning to Joe—"these here fellers what jines inter the army an' then comes home arter awhile without lief or license?"

"Deserters," replied Joe, simply.

"So fur, so good," said Mr. Pruitt. "Now, then, what do you call the fellers what jines inter the army arter they'er been told that their families'll be took keer of an' provided

fer by the rich folks at home; an' then, arter
they'er been in a right smart whet, they gits
word that their wives an' children is a lookin'
starvation in the face, an' stedder gittin' better
it gets wuss, an' bimeby they breaks loose an'
comes home? Now what sort er fellers do you
call them? Hold on!" exclaimed Mr. Pruitt, as
Joe was about to reply. " Wait! They hain't
got no money an' no niggers; they hain't got
nothin' but a little piece er lan'. They goes off
expectin' their wives'll be took keer of, an'
they comes home an' fines 'em in the last
stages. What sorter fellers do you call them?"

" Well," Joe replied, " I've never heard of
such a thing before."

" No," said Mr. Pruitt, " an' I'm mighty sorry
you've heard about it now. It ain't a purty
tale."

"Who are the men?" Joe asked.

" Yours, respectfully, John Pruitt an' Jeems
Wimberly, Ashbank deestrict, Hillsborough
Post-Office, State of Georgia," said Mr. Pruitt,
solemnly.

Joe had heard it hinted and rumored that
in some cases, especially where they lived remote from the relief committees, the families

of the soldiers were not so well provided for as they had a right to expect. He had even set up some editorials in *The Countryman* which hinted that there was suffering among the soldiers' wives and children; but he never dreamed that it was serious enough to create discontent among the soldiers. The story that Mr. Pruitt and his companion told amazed Joe Maxwell, but it need not be repeated here in detail. It amounted to this, that the two soldiers had deserted because their wives and children were suffering for food and clothing, and now they were fugitives.

CHAPTER X.

THE STORY-TELLERS.

THE strange company was silent for a long time. Mr. Pruitt and Mr. Wimberly sat with their elbows on their knees and their faces in their hands, and gazed into the fireplace, while the two negroes, true to their nature, began to nod as the talking ceased. The silence at last became painful to Joe Maxwell.

"Mink," he said, "suppose you should hear somebody coming, what would you do?"

"I wuz des worryin' 'bout dat 'while ago," replied the stalwart negro, passing his hand swiftly across his face. "I 'speck I'd be like de ole sheep you hear talk about in de tale."

"What was the tale?" asked Joe.

"Oh, 'tain't no long tale," said Mink. "One time dey wuz er ole sheep what had two chilluns. She call um up one day an' tell um dat dey better keep a sharp lookout whiles dey er eatin', kaze ef dey don't sumpin' n'er sholy gwine git um. Dey say 'Yessum,' an' dey went ter frolickin' up an' down de fiel'. Bimeby dey come runnin' back, an' 'low :

"'Oh, mammy, yon's a man! Mus' we-all run?'

"Dey went ter frolickin' up an' down de fiel'."

"Ole mammy sheep, she 'low: 'No! Go 'long and play.'

"Atter while, dey come runnin' back an' low: 'Mammy, mammy! yon's a hoss! Mus' we-all run?'

"Ole mammy sheep 'low: ''G'way frum here! Go on an' play.'

"Bimeby dey come runnin' back. 'Mammy, mammy! yon's a cow! Mus' we-all run?'

"Ole mammy sheep say: 'Go on an' play, an' quit yo' behavishness!'

"Atter while dey come runnin' back. 'Mammy! oh, mammy! yon's a dog! Mus' we-all run?'

"'Yes, yes! Run, chillun, run!'

"Dat de way wid me," said Mink. "Ef I wuz ter hear some un comin' I wouldn't know whedder ter set still an' nod, or whedder ter break an' run."

"That hain't much of a tale," remarked Mr. Pruitt, "but ther's a mighty heap er sense in it, shore."

"Shoo!" exclaimed Mink, "dat ain't no tale. You oughter hear dish yer Injun Bill tell um. He kin set up an' spit um out all night long. —Bill," said he, turning to his companion, "tell um dat un 'bout how de mountains come 'bout."

"Oh, I can't tell de tale," said Injun Bill, marking nervously in the floor with a splinter. "Ef I could tell dem like my daddy, den dat 'ud sorter be like sumpin'. Me an' my mammy come frum Norf Ca'liny. My daddy wuz Injun,

Ef you could hear him tell dem tales, he'd make you open yo' eyes."

" How wuz de mountains made, Bill? " asked Mink, after a pause.

" I wish I could tell it like my daddy," said Bill. " He wuz Cher'kee Injun, an' he know all 'bout it, kaze he say de Injuns wuz here long time fo' de white folks wuz, let 'lone de niggers.

" Well, one time dey wuz a great big flood. Hit rain so hard an' it rain so long dat it fair kivver de face er de yeth. Dey wuz lots mo' water dan what dey is in our kind er freshets, an' it got so atter while dat de folks had ter find some place whar dey kin stay, kaze ef dey don't dey all be drownded, dem an' de cree-turs, too.

" Well, one day de big Injun man call dem all up, an' say dey got ter move. So dey tuck der cloze an' der pots an' der pans an' foller 'long atter de big Injun, an' de creeters dey come 'long, too. Dey march an' dey march, an' bimeby dey come whar dey wuz a big hole in de groun'. Dey march in an' de big Injun he stay behine fer stop up de hole so de water can't leak in. 'Twant long 'fo' dey know dey wuz in de middle er de worl', deep down under de groun', an' dey had plenty room. Dey built der fires an' cook der vittles des same ez ef dey'd a been on top er de groun'.

"Dey stayed in dar I dunner how long, an' bimeby dey got tired er stayin' in dar, an' dey want ter come out. Some un um went off fer hunt fer de hole whar dey come in at, but dey can't fine it, an' den dey say dey skeered dey ain't never gwine ter git out. But de big Injun say dey plenty time, kaze fo' dey go out dey got ter know whedder de rain done stop. He say ef de smoke kin git out dey kin git out. Den dey ax 'im how he gwine fine out 'bout de rain, an' he say he gwine sen' some er de creeturs fer fine de hole whar de smoke go out, an' see 'bout de rain.

"Den de big Injun he went off by hisse'f an' study an' study how he gwine fine de hole whar de smoke go out. He sent de dog—de dog can't fine it. He sent de coon—de coon can't fine it. He sent de rabbit—de rabbit can't fine it. Den he went off by hisse'f an' study some mo', an' 'bout dat time de buzzud come 'long an' he ax de big Injun what make him look so lonesome. Den de big Injun tell de buzzud 'bout

"De buzzud ax de big Injun what make him look so lonesome."

'im tryin' fer fine de hole whar de smoke went fru. De buzzud he 'low dat him an' his ole 'oman kin fine it, an' den de big Injun tuck an' sent um off.

"Dey riz up, de buzzuds did, an' flewd de way de smoke went. Dey flewd up an' dey flewd down, an' dey flewd all 'roun' an' 'roun,' but dey ain't seed no hole whar de smoke go out at. Den dey come back, an' dis make de big Injun feel mo' lonesomer dan befo'. He study an' he study, un' bimeby he sent um out agin, an' tole um ter go high ez dey kin an' spy out de hole.

"So dey riz an' flewd up agin, an' dis time dey flewd right agin de top cr de yeth, up an' down an' 'roun' an' 'roun'. It bin rainin' so long dat de crust er de yeth wuz done wet plum fru, an' it wuz saft, an' when dey struck agin it dey made de print whar dey bin flyin'. Bimeby, de old man buzzud, he got mad, an' he sail 'roun' twel he git a good start, an' den he plow right 'long agin de roof. De ol' 'oman buzzud, she done de same, an' bimeby dey fine de hole whar de smoke went out. Dey peeped out, dey did, an' dey seed dat de rain done stop, but it monstus damp outside.

"Den dey went back an' de big Injun feel mighty good kaze dey done fine de hole. After so long a time he giv de word, an' dey all marched out fum de inside er de yeth an' went back ter whar dey useter live. It tuck um a mighty long time ter fine de place, kaze when dey went away de lan' wuz level, but when dey come back hit wuz full er hills an' mountains dat look like great big bumps an' long ridges. Dey ax dey se'f how come dis, an' dey study an' study. Bimeby de buzzud, he up'n say dat dem wuz de print he lef' when him an' his ole 'oman wuz a-flyin' roun' tryin' fer fine de hole whar de smoke went out. De groun' wuz saft, an' eve'y time de buzzuds 'ud fly agin it dey'd make hills an' mountains. Dat what my daddy say," said Injun Bill, decisively. "He wuz Injun man, an' he oughter know ef anybody do."

"What did I tell you?" exclaimed Mr. Wimberly, who, up to this time, had said nothing. "Mix Injun wi' nigger an' they hain't no kind er rigamarole they won't git up."

They all agreed, however, that Injun Bill's story was amusing, and after a while Mink said:

"I speck Marse John dar mought match dat tale ef he wuz ter try right hard."

Mr. Pruitt turned his pocket inside out to get some tobacco-crumbs for his pipe.

" Buddy," he remarked, turning to Joe Maxwell, "did you ever hear tell how the fox gits rid er fleas?"

Joe had never heard.

" Well," said Mr. Pruitt, " it's this away. When the fox, speshually ef it's one er these here big reds, gits full er fleas, which they er bleedze ter do in hot weather, he puts out an' goes tell he finds a flock er sheep. Then he runs in amongst 'em, an' runs along by the side er one tell he gits a chance ter pull a mouffle er wool out. Then he makes a break fer the creek an' finds him a wash-hole an' wades in.

" He don't, ez you may say, splunge in. He jest wades in, a little bit at a time. Fust he gits in up ter his knees, an' then he goes in deeper an' deeper. But he hain't in no hurry. When the water strikes the fleas, nachally they start fer high-water mark. The fox feels 'em crawl up, an' then he goes in a little deeper. When they crawl up ez high ez his back he goes in furder, an' then they crawl to'rds his head. He gits a little deeper, an' they crawl out on his nose.

Then he gits deeper, tell they hain't nothin' out er the water but the pint er his nose.

"Now all this time he's got that chunk er wool in his mouf, an' when the fleas hain't got nowheres else ter go they make fer that. Then when the fleas is all in the wool, the fox drops it in the water, comes out, shakes hisse'f, an' trots off ter do some other devilment."

"Dat cert'ny is one way fer ter git red er fleas," exclaimed Mink, laughing heartily. Then he turned to Injun Bill.

"Bill, what tale is dat I been hear you tell 'bout ole Brer Rabbit an' de overcoat? Dat ain't no nigger tale."

"Naw!" said Injun Bill, contemptuously. "Dat ain't no nigger tale. My daddy tell dat tale, an' he wa'nt no nigger. I wish I could tell it like I near him tell it."

"How did it go?" asked Mr. Wimberly.

"Well," said Injun Bill, rolling his eyes toward the rafters, "it sorter run dis way, nigh ez I kin reckermember: De time wuz when Mr. Beaver wuz de boss er all de creeturs. He wa'nt de biggest ner de strongest, but he wuz mighty smart. Fine cloze make fine folks in dem days, an' dat what Mr. Beaver had. Eve'y-body know him by his fine overcoat. He look slick all de week, an' he mighty perlite—he ain't never fergit his manners. Mr. Rabbit see all dis an' it make 'im feel jealous. He dunner how come Mr. Beaver kin be sech a big man, an' he study how he gwine make hisse'f populous wid de yuther creeturs.

"One time dey all make it up dat dey wuz gwine ter have a big meetin', an' so dey 'gun ter fix up. De word went 'roun' an' all de creeturs make ready ter come. Mr. Beaver he live up in de mountains, an' it wuz lots mo' dan a day's journey fum his house ter de place whar de creeturs gwine ter hol' der big meetin'. But he waz bleedze ter be dar, kaze he de head man. Ole Mr. Rabbit 'low ter hisse'f dat sumpin' got ter be done, an' dat mighty quick, an' so he put out fer Mr. Beaver house. Mr. Rabbit sho is a soon mover, mon, an' he git dar in little er no time. He say dey all so 'fraid Mr. Beaver ain't comin' ter de meetin' dat dey sont 'im atter 'im, an' he help Mr. Beaver pack his kyarpet-bag, an' went on back wid 'im fer comp'ny.

"Mr. Beaver can't git 'long ez peart ez Mr. Rabbit, kaze he so fat an' chunky, yit he don't lose no time; he des keep gwine fum sunup ter sundown. Des 'fo' dark dey come ter whar dey wuz a river, an' Mr. Rabbit, he 'low dey better camp out on de bank, an' git soon start in de mornin'. So dey built up a fier, an' cook der supper, an' 'bout de time dey wuz gittin' ready ter go ter bed Mr. Rabbit 'low:

"'Brer Beaver, I mighty feared we gwine ter have trouble dis night!' Mr. Beaver say, 'How comes so, Brer Rabbit?'

"Mr. Rabbit 'low: 'Dis country what we er in is called Rainin' Hot Embers, an' I don't like no sech name. Dat de reason I wanter stop close ter water.'

"Mr. Beaver ax, 'What de name er goodness we gwine do, Brer Rabbit?'

"Mr. Rabbit sorter scratch his head an' say, 'Oh, we des got ter put up wid it, an' do de bes' we kin.' Den he sorter study, an' 'low: 'I speck you better pull off dat fine overcoat er yourn, Brer Beaver, an' hang it up in de tree dar, kaze ef de wuss come ter de wuss, you sholy want ter save dat.'

"Den Mr. Beaver tuck off his overcoat an' hang it up in de tree, an' atter while dey lay down fer ter take a nap. Mr. Rabbit he stay wake, but twa'nt long 'fo' Mr. Beaver wuz done

gone ter sleep an' snorin' right along. He sno'
so loud dat Mr. Rabbit laugh ter hisse'f, an'
'low: 'Hey! Ole Brer Beaver pumpin' thun-
der fer dry wedder, but we gwine ter have
some rain, an' it'll be a mighty hot rain, mon.'

" Den Mr. Rabbit raise hisse'f on his elbow
an' look at Mr. Beaver. He soun' asleep, an' he
keep on a snorin'. Mr. Rabbit got up easy, an'
slipped roun' an' got 'im a great big piece er
bark, an' den he slip back ter de fier an' run de
piece er bark un' de hot embers des like it wuz
a shovel. He flung um up in de air, he did, an'
holler out:

" ' Run fer de water, Brer Beaver! run fer de
water! It's a rainin' hot embers! Run, Brer
Beaver! run!'

" De hot embers drapped on Mr. Beaver, an'
he scuffled 'bout mightily. Time Mr. Rabbit
hollered, he flung an'er shower er embers on 'im,
an' Mr. Beaver gun one loud squall an' splunged
inter de water head over heels. Mr. Rabbit
grab de fine overcoat an' run down de bank
twel he come ter whar dey wuz a canoe, an' he
got in dat an' went cross, an' den he put out ter
whar de creeturs gwine ter hol' der big meetin'.
Des 'fo' he got dar, he put on de overcoat, an'

he ain't do it none too soon, nudder, kaze some
un um had done got so unpatient 'long er waitin' fer Mr. Beaver dat dey went out on de road
a little fer ter meet 'im.

Brer Rabbit preaches.

" De overcoat wuz lots too big fer Mr. Rabbit, but it bin sech a long time sence de creeturs

had seed Mr. Beaver dat it look all right ter dem, an' so dey gallanted Mr. Rabbit ter de meetin'-place same like he wuz big man ez Mr. Beaver. Dey tuck 'im dar an' gallanted 'im up on de flatform, an' sot 'im down in de big cheer, an' made 'im de boss er de meetin'. Mr. Rabbit 'gun ter speak an' tell um he mighty much 'blige fer all deze favers, an' 'bout dat time Mr. Fox 'low:

"'Hey! Mr. Beaver done los' his voice!'

"Mr. Rabbit say he can't have no talkin', an' he kep on wid his speech. Bimeby Mr. Wolf say: 'Hey! Mr. Beaver bin sick, kaze his cloze ain't fit 'im.' Mr. Rabbit say he bleeze ter have order in de 'sembly, an' he go on wid his speech. 'Twan't long 'fo' Mr. Fox jump an' holler out:

"'Hey! Mr. Beaver done bought 'im some new years!'

"Mr. Rabbit cock up one eye, an' see dat bofe er his long years done come out fum un' de overcoat, an' den he know dat he better be gwine. He make er break, he did, an' bounced off'n de flatform, an' start fer de bushes, but some er de yuther creeturs head 'im off an' kotched 'im, an' den dey tuck 'im an' tried 'im, an' de jedge what sot on 'im say he mus' have mark on 'im so he can't fool um no mo'. Den dey tuck er sharp flint rock an' split his upper lip, an' dat how de rabbits is got der lip split."

"Shoo!" said Mink. "Dat Injun rabbit. Nigger rabbit would 'a' fooled dem creeturs right straight along, an' he wouldn't 'a' bin cotch, nudder."

"Jim," said Mr. Pruitt to Mr. Wimberly, "would it strain you too much ter whirl in an' tell us a tale? We wanter show this young un here that country folks hain't ez no 'count ez they look ter be."

"Jesso!" exclaimed Mr. Wimberly, with much animation. "I wuz jest a-thinkin' about one that popped in my min'. It ain't much of a tale, but it tickled me might'ly when I fust heard it, an' I hain't never fergot it."

"Well," said Mr. Pruitt, "out wi' it. It ain't nigh bedtime, an' ef it wuz we hain't got no beds ter go ter—that is, we hain't got none ter speak of."

"One time," Mr. Wimberly began, smacking his lips, "there wuz a man what took the idee that he had done gone an' larnt ever' blessid thing under the sun that thar' wuz ter larn, and

it worried him might'ly. He took the idee wi'
'im ever'whar he went. Folks called 'im Ole
Man Know-all. He sarched in ever' hole an'
cornder arter sump'n that he didn't know, but,
hunt whar he would an' when he might, he
couldn't fin' it. It looked like he know'd ever'-
thing ther' wuz an' had been. Nobody couldn't
tell 'im nothin' that he didn't know, an' it made
'im feel mighty lonesome. He studied an'
studied, an' at last he said ter hisse'f, sezee, that
ef thar' wan't nothin' more fer 'im ter larn, he
jest might ez well lay down an' die. He said
ter hisse'f, sezee, that may be Grandsir Death
could larn 'im sumpin. Jesso!

"Well, he went home one night an' built
'im up a big fire an' fixed his pallet an' lay
down. 'I won't lock the door,' sezee ; 'I'll
jist leave it onlatched so Grandsir Death can
come in, an' maybe he can larn me sump'n.'
Jesso!

"Ole Man Know-all lay thar on the pallet an'
waited. He'd doze a little an' then he'd wake
up, an' he rolled an' tossed about tell purty nigh
day. He wan't oneasy, so to speak, but he wuz
mighty restless. To'rds mornin' he heard some
un knock on his door—bam-bam! bam-bam! He

wan't skeered, but he got right weak. His mouth got dry, an' a big holler place come in his stomach. He sez ter hisse'f, sezee, 'Shorely that's Grandsir Death at the door.' Then he kivvered up his head an' shuck all over. 'Twan't long 'fo' the knock come agin :

"Bim-bim ! bim-bim ! bim !

"Ole Man Know-all thought his time wuz done come, certain an' shore, an' so he hollered :

"'Come in !'

"The door opened, but stedder it's bein' Grandsir Death it wuz a little nigger boy. Ole Man Know-all sez, sezee :

"'What you want this time er night?'

"The little nigger boy sez, sezee, 'Mammy sent me arter some fier.'

"Old Man Know-all told 'im ter come in an' git it. The little nigger boy went in an' started ter the fireplace.

"'They ain't no chunks thar,' sez Ole Man Know-all. 'Go git a shovel.'

"'Don't want no shovel,' sez the little nigger.

"'How you gwine ter take it?' sez Old Man Know-all.

" ' Easy enough,' sez the little nigger.

" Ole Man Know-all turned over an' watched 'im. He went ter the h'ath, filled the palm er one hand full er dead ashes, made a little nest in the middle, an' then picked up a fire-coal this way."

Suiting the action to the word, Mr. Wimberly picked up a glowing coal of fire, dropped it in the palm of his hand, whirled it around rapidly, and then neatly transferred it to the bowl of his pipe, where it lay glowing.

" The little nigger picked up the coal that way," Mr. Wimberly continued, " an' then hc started out. Ole Man Know-all hollered at 'im.

" ' Hol' on ! ' sezee ; ' how you gwine ter kindle a fire from jest one coal ? '

" ' Easy enough,' sez the little nigger.

" Ole Man Know-all jumped up an' follered 'im, an' when the little nigger come ter his mammy's house he got two fat pine splinters, picked up the coal er fire wi' 'em jest ez ef they'd 'a' been tongs, whirled it once-t er twice-t aroun' his head, an' thar wuz the blaze.

" ' Well,' sez Ole Man Know-all, ' I'm mighty glad Grandsir Death gimme the go-by last night, 'cause I've larnt sump'n new. An' I reckon, ef I keep my eyes open, I can larn lots more.' Jesso!"

"I've saw folks that thought they know'd it all," said Mr. Pruitt, "an' it most inginer'lly happens that all what they know wouldn't make the linin' fer a bug's nest."

There was some further talk, in which Joe Maxwell joined, or thought he did, and then the cabin and all its occupants seemed to fade before his eyes. He seemed, as in a dream, to hear Mr. Pruitt say that he wished to the Lord that his little boy was as healthy and as well fed as the boy from town, and Joe thought he heard the deserter telling his companions of the desperate condition in which he found his wife and two little children, who were living in a house remote from any settlement. The lad, much interested in this recital, opened his eyes to ask Mr. Pruitt some of the particulars, and, lo! it was morning. The fire was out, and the deserters and negroes had disappeared. In the east the sky glowed with the promise of the sun, the birds were singing in the old apple-trees, and the cows were lowing. In the distance Joe could hear the plow-hands singing as they rode to their tasks, and, when the sound of their song had died away, he thought he could hear, ever so faintly, the voice of Harbert calling his hogs.

Mink had told Joe where he was, and how to get home, and he had no difficulty in finding his way.

CHAPTER XI.

THE RELIEF COMMITTEE.

JOE MAXWELL was very tired the day after his experience in the cabin with the deserters and the runaways, but he was not too tired to joyfully accept an invitation to visit Hillsborough with the editor of *The Countryman*. For months the town had been practically in a state of siege. As the war progressed, it had been made a hospital station. The old temperance hall and many of the other buildings in the town had been fitted up for the accommodation of the sick and wounded. There were also many refugees in Hillsborough from Tennessee and north Georgia. While the town was crowded, the small-pox broke out, and for a month or more the country people were prevented from going there. Guards were placed on all the roads leading into the town; but this was not necessary, for the country people were not anxious to visit the place when they learned of the small-pox. Hillsborough was placed under martial law, and a provost-marshal given charge of affairs. This was necessary, not only to control the small-pox, but to control the convalescing soldiers, among whom were some very rough characters.

Joe had stayed away so long that the town seemed to be new to him. The playground in front of the old school-house was full of dingy hospital huts; the stores with which he had been familiar had been put to new and strange uses; and there were strange faces everywhere. Squads of soldiers were marching briskly here and there; men with crutches at their sides, or bandages on their heads, or with their arms in slings, were sunning themselves on every corner. Everything was strange. Even the old china-trees under which Joe had played hundreds of times had an unfamiliar look. Dazed and confused, the lad sat down on one of the long benches that were placed along the wall in front of some of the stores. The bench was tilted back against the wall, and one end of it was occupied by two men who were engaged in earnest conversation. Joe paid little attention to them at first, but a word or two that he heard caused him to observe them more closely. One of them was Mr. Deometari, the Greek exile and lawyer; the other was a man whom Joe did not know. He noticed that, although Mr. Deometari wore a faded and shabby uniform, his linen was spotless. His cuffs and shirt-bosom shone in the sun, and the setting of a heavy ring on his chubby finger sparkled like a star. "He has forgotten me," Joe thought, and he sat there determined not to make himself known, although he and Mr. Deometari had been great friends before the lad left Hillsborough.

"There's another thing I'm troubled about," Joe heard Mr. Deometari say to his companion. "Pruitt has come home."

"What's the matter with him?" asked the other.

"Deserted!" exclaimed Mr. Deometari.

"Well," said the other, "it's a big risk for a grown man to take. If he's caught, he'll have to pay the penalty."

"No!" exclaimed Mr. Deometari, bringing his fist down on his broad knee. "He'll be caught, but he won't pay the penalty."

"Why, what do you mean, Deo?" asked his companion.

"Don't you know him?" exclaimed Mr. Deometari. "He belongs to the Relief Committee!"

"Phew!" whistled the other, raising both his hands in the air, and letting them fall again.

"Don't you know him?" Deometari went on, with increasing earnestness. "He's the man that shot the otter."

Again Mr. Deometari's companion gave a long whistle of astonishment. "Jack Pruitt?" he asked.

"The identical man," said Deometari. "And do you know who this provost-marshal here is —this Captain Johnson?"

"Oh, yes," said the other; "he's the chap that stole the last dust of meal we had been saving to make soup for poor Tom Henderson."

"And what happened then?" inquired Mr. Deometari, as if trying to refresh his own memory instead of that of his companion. "Didn't Jack Pruitt give him a whipping?"

"Why, bless my life!" exclaimed the other. "What am I thinking about? Why, of course he did!" Saying this, Mr. Deometari's com-

panion rose to his feet, and caught sight of Joe
Maxwell as he did so.   Instantly he laid his hand
on Mr. Deometari's shoulder and remarked :

"It is fine weather for birds and boys."

Captain Johnson.

Joe was not at all disconcerted. He was
not eavesdropping, though he was very much
interested in what he had heard. The way to
interest a boy thoroughly is to puzzle him, and
Joe was puzzled.

"I saw Mr. Pruitt last night," he remarked,
and then, as his old friend turned, he said :

"How do you do, Mr. Deo? You haven't forgotten me, have you?"

Joe advanced and offered his hand. As Mr. Deometari took it, the frown cleared away from his face.

"Why, my dear boy!" he exclaimed, pulling the lad toward him and giving him a tremendous hugging, "I am delighted to see you! I could count on my ten fingers the people who are left to call me Deo. And if I counted, my boy, you may be sure I'd call your name long before I got to my little finger. Why, I'm proud of you, my boy! They tell me you write the little paragraphs in the paper credited to 'The Countryman's Devil'? Not all of them! Ah, well! it is honor enough if you only write some of them. Forget you, indeed!"

Mr. Deometari's greeting was not only cordial but affectionate, and the sincerity that shone in his face and echoed in his words brought tears to Joe Maxwell's eyes.

"Blandford," said Mr. Deometari, "you ought to know this boy. Don't you remember Joe Maxwell?"

"Why, yes!" said Mr. Blandford, showing

his white teeth and fixing his big black eyes on Joe. "He used to fight shy of me, but I remember him very well. He used to stand at the back of my chair and give me luck when I played draughts."

Mr. Blandford had changed greatly since Joe had seen him last. His black hair, which once fell over his shoulders in glossy curls, was now gray, and the curls were shorn away. The shoulders that were once straight and stalwart were slightly stooped. Of the gay and gallant young man whom Joe Maxwell had known as Archie Blandford nothing remained unchanged. except his brilliant eyes and his white teeth. Mr. Blandford had, in fact, seen hard service. He had been desperately shot in one of the battles, and had lain for months in a Richmond hospital. He was now, as he said, just beginning to feel his oats again.

"Come!" said Mr. Deometari, "we must go to my room. It is the same old room, in the same old tavern," he remarked.

When the two men and Joe Maxwell reached the room, which was one of the series opening on the long veranda of the old tavern, Mr. Deometari carefully closed the door, although the

weather was pleasant enough—it was the early
fall of 1864.

"Now, then," said he, drawing his chair
in front of Joe, and placing his hands on his
knees, "I heard you mention a name out
yonder when you first spoke to me.   What
was it?"

"Pruitt," said Joe.

"Precisely so," said Mr. Deometari, smiling
in a satisfied way.   "John Pruitt.   Now, what
did you say about John Pruitt?"

"Late of said county, deceased," dryly remarked Mr. Blandford, quoting from the form
of a legal advertisement.

"I said I saw him last night," said Joe, and
then he went on to explain the circumstances.

"Very good! and now what did you hear
me say about Pruitt?"

"You said he would be caught and not pun-
ished because he belonged to the Relief Committee."

"Hear that!" exclaimed Mr. Deometari.
"If any but these friendly ears had heard all
that, we'd have been put on Johnson's black list,
and maybe we'd have been transferred from the
black list to the guard-house.   Now, then," con-

tinued Mr. Deometari, "you don't know anything about the Relief Committee, of course, and
as you might be inquiring around about it, and
asking what John Pruitt, the deserter, has to do
with the Relief Committee, I'll tell you. But,
my dear boy, you must remember this : It's not a
matter to be joked about or talked of anywhere
outside of this room. Now, don't forget. It
isn't much of a secret; it is simply a piece of
business that concerns only a few people. Do
you remember reading or hearing about the retreat from Laurel Hill?" asked Mr. Deometari,
moving his chair back and unwinding the stem
of his Turkish pipe. "That was in the early
part of the war, and it will never cut much of a
figure in history, but some of those who were in
that retreat will never forget it. In the confusion of getting away a little squad of us, be-
longing mostly to the First Georgia Regiment,
were cut off from the main body. When we
halted to get our bearings there were not more
than a dozen of us."

"Seventeen, all told," remarked Mr. Blandford.

"Yes," said Mr. Deometari, "seventeen.
We were worse than lost. We were on the

mountains in a strange country. Behind us
was the enemy and before us was a forest of
laurel that stretched away as far as the eye
could reach. To the right or to the left was
the same uncertainty. We could hear nothing
of the rest of the command. To fire a gun was
to invite capture, and there was nothing for us
to do but push ahead through the scrubby
growth."

" The commissary was absent on a furlough,"
remarked Mr. Blandford.

" Yes," said Mr. Deometari, laughing. " The
commissary was missing, and rations were
scanty. Some of the men had none at all.
Some had a little hard-tack, and others had a
handful or so of meal. Though the weather was
bitter cold, we built no fire the first night, for
fear of attracting the attention of the enemy.
The next day and the next we struggled on.
We saved our rations the best we could, but
they gave out after a while, and there was nothing left but a little meal which John Pruitt was
saving up for Tom Henderson, who was ill and
weak with fever. Every day, when we'd stop to
breathe awhile, Pruitt would make Henderson
a little cupful of gruel, while the rest of us ate

corn, or roots, or chewed the inside bark of the trees."

"And nobody begrudged Tom his gruel," said Mr. Blandford, "though I'll swear the sight of it gave me the all-overs."

"Oh, yes!" exclaimed Mr. Deometari. "Somebody did begrudge Tom the gruel. One night this Captain Johnson, who is lording it around here now, thought Pruitt and the rest of us were asleep, and he made an effort to steal the little meal that was left. Well, Pruitt was very wide awake, and he caught Johnson and gave him a tremendous flogging; but the villain had already got into the haversack, and in the struggle the meal was spilled."

Mr. Deometari coiled the stem of his pipe around his neck, and blew a great cloud of smoke toward the ceiling.

"But what about the Relief Committee, Mr. Deo?" inquired Joe.

"Why, to be sure! A nice story-teller am I!" exclaimed Mr. Deometari. "I had forgotten the Relief Committee entirely. Well, we went forward, growing weaker and weaker every day, until finally we came to a ravine."

" It was a gorge," observed Mr. Blandford, stretching himself out on Mr. Deometari's bed, " and a deep one too."

" Yes, a gorge," said Mr. Deometari. " When we reached that gorge we were in a famished

Some of the men dropped on the ground and declared that they would go no farther.

condition. Not a bird could be seen except crows and buzzards. The crows would have made good eating, no doubt, but they were

very shy. We had lived in the hope of finding a hog, or a sheep, or a cow, but not a sign
of a four-footed creature did we see. I don't
know how it was, but that gorge seemed to
stretch across our path like the Gulf of Despair. Some of the men dropped on the ground
and declared that they would go no farther.
They said they had no desire to live; they were
as weak and as foolish as children. Of the seventeen men in the squad, there were but five
who had any hope, any spunk, or any spirit—
Blandford there, Pruitt, Henderson, this Captain
Johnson, and myself."

"You ought to put yourself first," said Mr.
Blandford. "You were as fat as a pig all the
time, and as full of life as a grasshopper in
July."

"This ravine or gorge," continued Mr.
Deometari, paying no attention to the interruption, "was our salvation. Mr. Blandford
and Pruitt explored it for a little distance, and
they found a little stream of water running at
the bottom. It was what you call a branch.
When they came back there was considerable
disagreement among the men. The poor creatures, weak and irritable from hunger, had lost

all hope, and would listen to no argument that didn't suit their whims. There was this question to settle: Should we cross the gorge and continue in the course we had been going, or should we follow the gorge? It was a very serious question. We had not the slightest idea where we were. We had been wandering about in the mountains for eight days, and if we were going to get out at all it was necessary to be in a hurry about it.

"Then there was another question. If the gorge was to be followed, which way should we go? Should we follow the running water or should we go the other way? Blandford and Pruitt had already made up their minds to follow the running water, and of course I was going with them."

"That's because it was down hill," remarked Mr. Blandford, laughing. "Deo always said his legs were never made for going up hill."

"We had a great discussion. My dear boy, if you want to see how peevish and ill-natured and idiotic a grown man can be, just starve him for a matter of eight or nine days. Some wanted to go one way and some wanted to go another, while others wanted to stay where they were. Actually, Blandford and I had to cut hickories and pretend that we were going to flog the men who wanted to stay there and die, and when we got them on their feet we had to drive them along like a drove of sheep, while Pruitt led the way.

"Pruitt's idea was that the running water led somewhere. This may seem to be a very simple matter now, but in our weak and confused condition it was a very fortunate thing that he had the idea and stuck to it. We found out afterward that if we had continued on the course we had been going, or if we had followed the gorge in the other direction, we would have buried ourselves in a wilderness more than a hundred miles in extent.

"The next day a couple of hawks and two jay-birds were shot, and, though they made small rations for seventeen men, yet they were refreshing, and the very sight of them made us feel better. The walls of the gorge grew wider apart, and the branch became larger as we followed it. The third day after we had changed our course Pruitt, who was ahead, suddenly paused and lifted his hand. Some of the men were so weak that they swayed from side to side as they halted. The sight of them was pitiful. We soon saw what had attracted Pruitt's attention. On the rocks, above a pool of water, an otter lay sunning himself. He was as fat as butter. We stood speechless a moment and then sank to the ground. There was no fear that the otter could hear our voices, for the branch, which had now grown into a creek, fell noisily into the pool. If he had heard us —if he had slipped off the rocks and disappeared—" Mr. Deometari paused and looked into his pipe.

"Great heavens, Deo!" exclaimed Mr. Blandford, jumping up from the bed. "I'll never forget that as long as I live! I never had such feelings before, and I've never had such since."

"Yes," continued Mr. Deometari, "it was an awful moment. Each man knew that we must have the otter, but how could we get him? He must be shot, but who could shoot him? Who would have nerve enough to put the ball in the right spot? The man who held the gun would know how much depended on him; he would be too excited to shoot straight. I looked at the men, and most of them were

trembling. Those who were not trembling
were as white as a sheet with excitement. I
looked at Pruitt, and he was standing up, watching the otter, and whistling a little jig under
his breath. So I said to him, as quietly as I
could :

"'Take your gun, man, and give it to him.
You can't miss. He's as big as a barn-door.'

"Pruitt dropped on one knee, put a fresh
cap on his gun, shook his hand loose from his
sleeve, leveled his piece, and said, 'Pray for it,
boys!' Then he fired. He was so weak that
the gun kicked him over. When I looked at
the otter it seemed that the creature had never
moved, but presently I saw a leg quivering, and
then we rushed forward as fast as we could, the
happiest lot of men you ever saw on this earth.
The otter was shot through the head. The
men were so ravenous they acted like maniacs.
It was all that Blandford and Pruitt and I
could do to keep them from falling on the otter
with their knives and eating it raw, hide and
all.

"But it saved us," Mr. Deometari went on,
"and we had something to spare. The next
day we met with a farmer hunting his stray

"Pray for it, boys!"

sheep, and we soon got back to the army. Four of us formed the Relief Committee before we parted. Blandford, Pruitt, Tom Henderson, and myself—the men who had never lost hope —promised each other, and shook hands on it, that whenever one got in trouble the others would help him out without any questions.

" Now, it isn't necessary to ask any questions about Pruitt. He deserted because his family were in a starving condition."

" Yes," said Mr. Blandford, bringing his heavy jaws together with a snap, " and I believe in my soul that Johnson has kept food and clothes away from them ! "

" I know he has," said Mr. Deometari, calmly. " Tom Henderson is one of Johnson's clerks, and he keeps the run of things. He is to meet us to-night, and then you'll see a man who has been blazing mad for three months.—Now, my boy," continued Mr. Deometari, " forget all about this. You are too young to be troubled with such things. We're just watching to see how Captain Johnson proposes to pay off the score he owes Pruitt. Should you chance to see John, just tell him that the Relief Committee has taken charge of Hillsborough for a few weeks. Another thing," said Mr. Deometari, laying his hand kindly on the boy's shoulder, "if you should be sent for some day or some night, just drop everything and come with the messenger. A bright chap like you is never too small to do good."

The two men shook hands with Joe, and Mr. Blandford gravely took off his hat when he bade the boy good-by.

CHAPTER XII.

A GEORGIA FOX-HUNT.

FOR a few days Joe Maxwell forgot all about Mr. Deometari, Mr. Blandford, and Mr. Pruitt. There was distinguished company visiting the editor of *The Countryman*—a young lady from Virginia, Miss Nellie Carter, and her mother, and some young officers at home on furlough. One of these young officers, a kinsman of the editor, brought his pack of fox-hounds, and arrangements were made for a grand fox-hunt. The plantation seemed to arouse itself to please the visitors. The negroes around the house put on their Sunday clothes and went hurrying about their duties, as if to show themselves at their best.

Joe was very glad when the editor told him that he was to go with the fox-hunters and act as master of ceremonies. Fox-hunting was a sport of which he was very fond, for it seemed to combine all the elements of health and pleasure in outdoor life. Shortly after Joe went to the plantation the editor of *The Countryman* had brought from Hillsborough a hound puppy, which had been sent him by a Mr. Birdsong. This Mr. Birdsong was a celebrated breeder of fox-hounds, having at one time the only pack south of Virginia that could catch a red fox. He was a great admirer of the editor of *The Countryman*, and he sent him the dog as a gift. In his letter Mr. Birdsong wrote that the puppy had been raised under a gourd-vine, and so the editor called him Jonah. Joe Maxwell thought the name was a very good one, but it turned out that the dog was very much better than his name. The editor gave the dog to Joe, who took great pains in training him. Before Jonah was six months old he had learned to trail a fox-skin, and by the time he was a year old hardly a morning passed that Joe did not drag the skin for the pleasure of seeing Jonah trail it. He developed great speed and powers of scent, and he was not more than two years old before he had run down and caught a red fox, unaided and alone. Naturally, Joe was very proud of Jonah, and he was glad of an opportunity to show off the dog's hunting qualities.

In training Jonah, Joe had also unwittingly trained an old fox that made his home on the plantation. The fox came to be well known to every hunter in the county. He was old, and tough, and sly. He had been pursued so often that if he heard a dog bark in the early morning hours, or a horn blow, he was up and away. The negroes called him " Old Sandy," and this was the name he came to be known by. Jonah when a puppy had trailed Old Sandy many a time, and Joe knew all his tricks and turnings. He decided that it would be well to give the young officer's pack some exercise with this cunning old fox.

All the arrangements for the hunt were made by the editor. Joe Maxwell was to escort Miss Nellie Carter, who, although a Virginian and a good horsewoman, had never ridden across the country after a fox. The lad was to manage so that Miss Carter should see at least as much of the hunt as the young men who were to follow the hounds, while Harbert was to go along to pull down and put up the fences. To Joe this was a new and comical feature of fox-hunting, but the editor said that this would be safer for Miss Carter.

When the morning of the hunt arrived, Joe was ready before any of the guests, as he had intended to be. He wanted to see to everything, much to Harbert's amusement. Like all boys, he was excited and enthusiastic, and he was very anxious to see the hunt go off successfully. Finally, when all had had a cup of coffee, they mounted their horses and were ready to go.

"Now, then," said Joe, feeling a little awkward and embarrassed, as he knew that Miss Nellie Carter was looking and listening, "there must be no horn-blowing until after the hunt is over. Of course, you can blow if you want to," Joe went on, thinking he had heard one of the young men laugh, "but we won't have much of a hunt. We are going after Old Sandy this morning, and he doesn't like to hear a horn at all. If we can keep the dogs from barking until we get to the field, so much the better."

"You must pay attention," said Miss Carter, as some of the young men were beginning to make sarcastic suggestions. "I want to see a real fox-hunt, and I'm sure it will be better to follow Mr. Maxwell's advice."

Joe blushed to here his name pronounced so sweetly, but in the dim twilight of morning his embarrassment could not be seen.

"Are your dogs all here, sir?" he asked the young man who had brought his hounds. "I have counted seven, and mine makes eight."

"Is yours a rabbit-dog?" the young man asked.

"Oh, he's very good for rabbits," replied Joe, irritated by the question.

"Then hadn't we better leave him?" the young man asked, not unkindly. "He might give us a good deal of trouble."

"I'll answer for that," said Joe. "If everybody is ready, we'll go."

"You are to be my escort, Mr. Maxwell," said Miss Carter, taking her place by Joe's side, "and I know I shall be well taken care of."

The cavalcade moved off and for a mile followed the public road. Then it turned into a lane and then into a plantation road that led to what was called the "Turner old field," where for three or four years, and perhaps longer, Old Sandy had made his headquarters. By the time the hunters reached the field,

which was a mile in extent, and made up
of pasture-land overgrown with broom-sedge,
wild plum-trees, and blackberry-vines, the
dawn had disappeared before the sun. Red
and yellow clouds mingled together in the
east, and a rosy glow fell across the hills and
woods. As they halted for Harbert to take
down the fence, Joe stole a glance at his companion, and as she sat with her lips parted
and the faint reflection of the rosy sky on her
cheeks, he thought he had never seen a pret-
tier picture. Jonah seemed to be of the same
opinion, for he stood by the young lady's horse,
looking into her face, and whistled wistfully
through his nose.

" That is your dog, I know !" said Miss Carter. " Why, he's a perfect beauty ! Poor fellow !" she exclaimed, stretching her arm out
and filliping her fingers. Jonah gathered himself together, leaped lightly into the air, and
touched her fair hand with his velvet tongue.
Joe blushed with delight. " Why, he jumped
as high as a man's head !" she cried. " I know
he will catch the fox."

" I think we have stolen a march on Old
Sandy," said Joe, " and if we have, you'll see

a fine race. I hope the other dogs can keep up."

"Ah," said their owner, "they are Maryland dogs."

"My dog," said Joe, proudly, "is a Bird-song."

By this time the hunters had crossed the fence, and the dogs, with the exception of Jonah, were beginning to cast about in the broom-sedge and brier-patches.

"I hope Jonah isn't lazy," said Miss Carter, watching the dog as he walked in quiet dignity by the side of her horse.

"Oh, no," said Joe, "he isn't lazy; but he never gets in a hurry until the time comes."

The young men tried to tease Joe about Jonah, but the lad only smiled, and Jonah gradually worked away from the horses. It was noticed that he did not hunt as closely as the other dogs, nor did he nose the ground as carefully. He swept the field in ever-widening circles, going in an easy gallop, that was the perfection of grace, and energy, and strength. Presently Harbert cried out:

"Looky yonder, Marse Joe! Looky yonder at Jonah!"

All eyes were turned in the direction that
Harbert pointed. The dog was hunting where
the brown sedge was higher than his head, and
he had evidently discovered something, for he
would leap into the air, look around, and drop
back into the sedge, only to go through the
same performance with increasing energy.

"Why don't he give a yelp or two and call
the other dogs to help him?" exclaimed one of
the young men.

"He's no tattler," said Joe, "and he doesn't
need any help. That fox has either just got up
or he isn't twenty yards away. Just wait!"

The next moment Jonah gave tongue with
thrilling energy, repeated the challenge twice,
and was off, topping the fence like a bird. The
effect on the other dogs was magical; they
rushed to the cry, caught up the red-hot drag,
scrambled over the fence the best they could,
and went away, followed by a cheer from Harbert that shook the dew from the leaves. The
young men were off, too, and Joe had all he
could do to hold his horse, which was in the
habit of running with the hounds. The sound
of the hunt grew fainter as the dogs ran across
a stretch of meadow-land and through a skirt of

woods to the open country beyond ; and Joe and Miss Carter, accompanied by Harbert, proceeded leisurely to the brow of a hill near by.

" If that is Old Sandy," said Joe, " he will come across the Bermuda field yonder, turn to the left, and pass us not very far from that dead pine." Joe was very proud of his knowledge.

" Why, we shall see the best of the hunt!" cried Miss Carter, enthusiastically.

They sat on their horses and listened. Sometimes the hounds seemed to be coming nearer, and then they would veer off. Finally, their musical voices melted away in the distance. Joe kept his eyes on the Bermuda field, and so did Harbert, while Miss Carter tapped her horse's mane gently with her riding-whip, and seemed to be enjoying the scene. They waited a long time, and Joe was beginning to grow disheartened, when Harbert suddenly exclaimed :

" Looky yonder, Marse Joe ! what dat gwine 'cross de Bermuda pastur' ? "

Across the brow of the hill slipped a tawny shadow—slipped across and disappeared before Miss Carter could see it.

" That's Old Sandy," cried Joe ; " now watch for Jonah ! "

Presently the hounds could be heard again, coming nearer and nearer. Then a larger and a darker shadow sprang out of the woods and swept across the pasture, moving swiftly and yet with the regularity of machinery. At short intervals a little puff of vapor would rise from this black shadow, and then the clear voice of Jonah would come ringing over the valley. Then the rest of the dogs, a group of shadows, with musical voices, swept across the Bermuda field.

"Oh, how beautiful!" exclaimed Miss Carter, clapping her little hands.

"Wait," said Joe; "don't make any noise. He'll pass here, and go to the fence yonder, and if he isn't scared to death you'll see a pretty trick."

It was a wide circle the fox made after he passed through the Bermuda field. He crossed the little stream that ran through the valley, skirted a pine thicket, ran for a quarter of a mile along a plantation path, and then turned and came down the fallow ground that lay between the creek and the hill where Joe and Miss Carter, with Harbert, had taken their stand. It was a comparatively level stretch of nearly a half-mile. The old corn-rows ran lengthwise the field, and down one of these Old Sandy came in full view of those who were waiting to see him pass. He was running rapidly, but not at full speed, and, although his tongue was hanging out, he was not distressed. Reaching the fence two hundred yards away from the spectators, he clambered lightly to the top, sat down on a rail and began to lick his fore-paws, stopping occasionally, with one paw suspended in the air, to listen to the dogs. In a moment or two more Jonah entered the field at the head of the valley. Old Sandy, carefully balancing himself on the top rail of the fence, walked it for a hundred yards or more, then gathering himself together sprang into the air and fell in the broomsedge fully twenty feet away from the fence.

"Oh, I hope the dogs won't catch him!" exclaimed Miss Carter. "He surely deserves to escape!"

"He got sense like folks," said Harbert.

"He stayed on the fence too long. Just look at Jonah!" cried Joe.

The hound came down the field like a whirlwind. He was running at least thirty yards to the left of the furrow the fox had followed.

" Why, he isn't following the track of the fox," exclaimed Miss Carter. " I thought hounds trailed foxes by the scent."

" They do," said Joe, " but Jonah doesn't need to follow it as the other dogs do. The dog that runs with his nose to the ground can never catch a red fox."

"Isn't he beautiful ! " cried the young lady, as Jonah rushed past, his head up and his sonorous voice making music in the air. He topped the fence some distance above the point where the fox had left it, lost the trail, and made a sweeping circle to the right, increasing his speed as he did so. Still at fault, he circled widely to the left, picked up the drag a quarter of a mile from the fence, and pushed on more eagerly than ever. The rest of the dogs had overrun the track at the point where the fox had turned to enter the field, but they finally found it again, and went by the spectators in fine style, running together very prettily. At the fence they lost the trail, and for some minutes they were casting about. One of the younger dogs wanted to take the back track, but Harbert turned him around, and was about to set the pack right, when the voice of Jonah was heard again, clear and ringing. Old Sandy, finding himself hard pushed, had dropped flat in the grass and allowed the hound to overrun him. Then he doubled, and started back. He gained but little, but he was still game. Jonah whirled in a short circle, and was after the fox almost instantly. Old Sandy seemed to know that this was his last opportunity. With a marvelous burst of speed he plunged through the belated dogs that were hunting for the lost drag, slipped through the fence, and went back by the spectators like a flash. There was a tremendous outburst of music from the dogs as they sighted him, and for one brief moment Joe was afraid that Jonah would be thrown out. The next instant the dog appeared on the fence, and there he sighted the fox. It was then that the courage and speed of Jonah showed themselves. Nothing could have stood up before him. Within a hundred yards he ran into the fox. Realizing his fate, Old Sandy leaped into the air with a squall, and the next moment the powerful jaws of Jonah had closed on him.

By this time the rest of the hunters had come in sight. From a distance they witnessed the catch. They saw the rush that Jonah made;

they saw Miss Carter and Joe Maxwell galloping forward ; they saw the lad leap from his
horse and bend over the fox, around which the
dogs were jumping and howling ; they saw him
rise, with hat in hand, and present something to

Old Sandy leaped into the air.

his fair companion ; and then they knew that
the young lady would ride home with Old
Sandy's brush suspended from her saddle.

These hunters came up after a while. Their
horses were jaded, and the riders themselves
looked unhappy.

" Did you notice which one of my dogs

caught the fox?" asked the young man to whom the pack belonged.

" No, sir, I did not," said Joe.

" I declare that is too funny!" exclaimed Miss Carter, laughing merrily, and then she went on to describe the chase as she saw it. The young man smiled as though he thought it was all a joke, and that night he called up Harbert, and offered him a dollar in Confederate money if he would tell the truth about the matter. Harbert told him the truth, but it was so unpleasant that the young man forgot all about the money, although a dollar at that time was worth not more than twelve and a half cents.

Miss Carter seemed to be almost as proud of Jonah's performance as Joe was, and this made the lad feel very proud and happy. But, as they were going home, an incident happened which, for the time, and for some days afterward, drove all thoughts of Jonah and fox-hunting out of his mind. The hunters went back the way they had come, and shortly after they entered the public road they met a small procession that turned out to be very interesting, especially to Joe. First, there was a spring wagon, drawn by one horse and driven by a

negro. On the seat with the negro, and se-
curely fastened with ropes, was Mr. John Pruitt,
the deserter. Behind the negro and Mr. Pruitt
were two soldiers with guns, and three soldiers
mounted on horses, and armed, acted as escort.
The young officers who had been hunting with
Joe Maxwell stopped the wagon and made in-
quiries until they had satisfied their curiosity.
Joe would have spoken to Mr. Pruitt, but the
latter, by an almost imperceptible movement of
the head, seemed to forbid it. His face was as
serene as if he had been on dress parade. As
the wagon was about to move on, he spoke:

"Ain't that the young chap that works in
the printin'-office down by Phœnix school-
house?" he asked, nodding his head toward
Joe, without looking at him.

"Yes," said one of the young officers.

"Well, sir," said Mr. Pruitt, drawing a long
breath, "I wish you'd please tell him to be so
good ez to git word to my wife down in the
Yarberry settlement that I won't have a chance
to come home in a week or more, an' she'll
hafter do the best she kin tell I git back."

Joe said he would be glad to do so.

"I 'low'd he would," said Mr. Pruitt, still

speaking to the young officer; "an' I'm mighty much erbliged."

Then the little procession moved on toward Hillsborough, and the hunters went homeward. Miss Nellie Carter was very much interested.

"He doesn't look a bit like a deserter," she said, impulsively, "and I'm sure there's some mistake. I don't believe a deserter could hold his head up."

Joe then made bold to tell her what he had heard—that Mr. Pruitt and several other soldiers had come home because they heard their families were suffering for food. Miss Carter was very much interested, and wanted to go with the lad to visit Mrs. Pruitt.

"But I can't go," said Joe; "there's nobody to do my work in the printing-office. I'll send Mrs. Pruitt word to-night by some of the negroes."

"No, no!" cried Miss Carter, "that will never do. I'll see my cousin and tell him about it. You must go to-day, and I'll go with you. Oh, it mustn't be postponed; you must go this very afternoon! Why, what is this little newspaper you are printing out here in the woods? The woman may be suffering."

Miss Carter saw her cousin, the editor, and lost no time in telling him about Mr. Pruitt and his family. The editor, who was one of the best of men, was so much interested that, instead of sending Joe with the young lady, he went himself, taking in his buggy a stout hamper of provisions. When they came back, Miss Carter's eyes were red, as if she had been crying, and the editor looked very serious.

"I'm very glad you didn't go," he said to Joe, when Miss Carter had disappeared in the house.

"Was anybody dead?" asked Joe.

"No," replied the editor. "Oh, no; nothing so bad as that. But the woman and her children have been in a terrible fix! I don't know who is to blame for it, but I shall score the county officers and the Ladies' Aid Society in the next paper. These people have been actually in a starving condition, and they look worse than if they had gone through a spell of fever. They are nothing but skin and bones. The main trouble is that they live in such an out-of-the-way place. The house is a mile from the public road, and hard to find."

"I heard," said Joe, "that the provost-marshal had something to do with holding back supplies that ought to have gone to Mr. Pruitt's family."

"How could he?" asked the editor; and then he added, quickly: "Why, of course he could; he is in charge of everything. He is judge, jury, lawyer, and general dictator. Who told you about it?"

"I heard it in town," said Joe.

"Well, he's a mean rascal," said the editor. He bade Joe good-evening, and started in the house, but half-way up the steps he paused and called to the lad.

"Here's something I forgot to ask you about," he said, taking a letter from his pocket. "It is a note from Deo about you. What do you know about Deo?"

"About me?" said Joe. "I used to know Mr. Deo when I was a little boy."

"Well, you are not such a big boy now," said the editor, smiling. "Here is what Deo says: 'You have a boy working in your print-ing-office who can make himself very useful in a good cause when the time comes. His name is Joe Maxwell, and he is a very good friend of mine. At least he used to be. Before long I shall send for him, and, whether I send in the day or in the night, I want you to let him come. If I were to tell you now what I want with him, you would laugh and say that all fat men are foolish. What I want him to do can be done only by a woman or a boy. A woman is not to be thought of, and I know of no boy I can trust except Maxwell. Just give him your permission beforehand, so that there will be no delay.' Now what do you think about it?" inquired the editor.

"May I go?" asked Joe.

"That is for you to decide," said the editor. "I have been knowing Deometari for nearly twenty years. He's a good lawyer and a clever man. But, if you do go, be careful of yourself. Don't get into any trouble. Tell Deo that all of us like you out here, and we don't want any foolishness."

CHAPTER XIII.

A NIGHT'S ADVENTURES.

IT was the very next afternoon that Joe Maxwell received the expected summons from Mr. Deometari. The message was brought by a negro on a mule, and the mule seemed to be very tired, although it had come only nine miles.

"I never is see no mule like dis," said the negro, indignantly, as he took a soiled letter from his hat and handed it to Joe. "I start from town at two o'tlocks, an' here 'tis mos' night. I got me a stick an' I hit 'er on one side, an' den she'd shy on t'er side de road, an' when I hit 'er on dat side, she'd shy on dis side. She been gwine slonchways de whole blessed way."

Mr. Deomatari's note had neither address nor signature, and it was very brief. "Come at once," it said. "You remember the re-

treat from Laurel Hill and the otter? Come
in by the jail and around by the Branham

The messenger.

place. If some one cries, ' Who goes there?'
say, ' It is the Relief.' "

Joe turned the note over and studied it.

" Who gave you this?" he asked the negro.

" Dat chuffy-lookin' white man what stay dar
at de tavern.   He say you mustn't wait for me,
but des push on.   Dem wuz his ve'y words—
des push on."

Joe had some trouble in getting away.   The
editor had gone off somewhere in the plantation; and Butterfly, the horse he proposed to
ride—the horse he always rode—was in the
pasture, and a colt in a plantation pasture is as
big a problem as a hard sum in arithmetic.   The
colt is like the answer.   It is there somewhere;
but how are you going to get it, and when?
Harbert solved the problem after a while by
cornering the colt and catching him; but the
sun was nearly down when Joe started, and he
then had nine miles to ride.   Harbert, who was
a sort of plantation almanac, said there would
be no moon until after midnight, and a mighty
small one then; but this made no difference to
Joe Maxwell.   Every foot of the road was as
familiar to him as it was to old Mr. Wall, the
hatter, who was in the habit of remarking that,
if anybody would bring him a hatful of gravel
from the big road that led to Hillsborough, he'd
" up an' tell 'em right whar they scooped it up
at."   Joe not only knew the road well, but he

was well mounted. Butterfly had all the faults of a colt except fear. He was high-spirited and nervous, but nothing seemed to frighten him. When the lad started, Harbert ran on ahead to unlatch the big plantation gate that opened on the public road.

"Good-night, Marse Joe," said the negro. "I wish you mighty well."

"Good-night, Harbert," responded Joe, as he went cantering into the darkness.

There was something more than a touch of fall in the evening air, and Butterfly sprang forward eagerly, and chafed at the bit that held him back. The short, sharp snorts that came from his quivering nostrils showed the tremendous energy he had in reserve, and it was not until he had gone a mile or more that he settled down into the long, swift, sweeping gallop that seemed in the dim light to throw the trees and fences behind him. At a cross-road Joe heard the tramp of horses and the jingling of spurs and bridle-bits, but he never paused, and it was not until long afterward he learned that he had come near forming the acquaintance of Wilson's raiders, who were making their way back to Atlanta.

By the time the stars had come out, Joe could see the lights of Hillsborough twinkling in the distance, and in a short time he had turned into the back street that led by the jail and made way across the town until he reached the square below the tavern. Then he turned to the left, and was soon in front of Mr. Deometari's room. Boy-like, he was secretly sorry that some sentinel had not challenged him on the way, so that he could give the countersign. A muffled figure, sitting on the edge of the veranda, roused itself as Joe rode up.

"Where is Mr. Deometari?" the lad asked.

"He in dar," replied the figure. "Is you fum de plantation, sah?"

"Yes."

"Den I'm to take yo' hoss," the negro said.

"Well, you must be careful with him," said the lad.

"Dat I will, suh, kaze Marse Deo say he gwine pay me, an', 'sides dat, I stays at de liberty stable."

Joe saw his horse led away, and then he knocked at Mr. Deometari's door.

"Come in!" cried that genial gentleman.

"I'm here, sir," said Joe, as he entered.

"Why, my dear boy! so you are! and glad I am to see you. And you are on time. I had just pulled out my watch, and said to myself, 'In one short quarter of an hour the boy should be here, and I shall have his supper ready for him.' And just then you knocked, and here is my watch still in my hand. My dear boy, sit down and rest your bones. I feel better."

Mr. Deomatari had supper for Joe and himself brought to his room, and as he ate he talked.

"You are a clever chap," said Mr. Deometari. "You don't know how clever you are. No," he went on, seeing a curious smile on Joe's face—"no, I'm not making fun of you. I mean just what I say. Where is the boy in this town who would have galloped through the dark on an errand that he knew nothing of? I tell you, he is not to be found. But suppose he could be found, wouldn't he bother me with ten thousand questions about what he was expected to do, and how he was going to do it, and when, and which, and what not? Now, I want to ask you why you came?"

"Because you sent for me," said Joe buttering another biscuit. "And because I wanted to find out all about—"

" All about what? " asked Mr. Deometari.

" About Mr. Pruitt, and—everything."

" Well," said Mr. Deometari, " I won't tell
you precisely why I sent for you—you'll find
out for yourself; but one of the reasons is that
I want you to go with a little party of us to a
point not far from your home. You know the
roads, and you know what the negroes call the
short cuts."

" To-night? " asked Joe.

" Yes, to - night.   Not now, but a little
later."

Joe ate his supper, and then sat gazing into
the fire that had been kindled on the hearth.

" I was just thinking, Mr. Deo," he said,
after a while, " whether I ought to go and see
mother."

" Now that is the question."   Mr. Deometari drew his chair closer to the lad, as if
preparing to argue the matter. " Of course,
you feel as if you ought to go.   That is natural
But, if you go, you will have to give your
mother some reason for being here.   You could
only tell her that I had sent for you.   This is
such a poor reason that she would be uneasy.
Don't you think so ? "

" Well," said Joe, after a pause, " I can come to see her next Sunday."

Rubbing his fat hands together, Mr. Deometari looked at Joe a long time. He seemed to be meditating. The ring on his finger glistened like a ray of sunlight that had been captured and was trying to escape.

" I want to take you around," hc said to Joe after a while, " and introduce you to Captain Johnson, our worthy provost-marshal."

" Me? " asked the lad, in a tone of astonishment.

" Yes," said Mr. Deometari. " Why not? A bright boy like you should be acquainted with all our great military men. Our noble captain would be very glad to see you if he knew as much about your visit as I do."

" But as it is," said Joe, quickly, " he doesn't know any more about it than I do."

" My dear boy," exclaimed Mr. Deometari, in a bantering tone, " don't get impatient. It is so very simple that all our plans might be spoiled if I told you. Now, then," he continued, looking at his watch, " if you are ready, we will go. You have no overcoat, but my shawl here will answer just as well."

Joe protested that he never wore an overcoat, even in the coldest weather; but his pro-
test had no effect on Mr. Deometari, who gave
the shawl a dexterous turn and wrapped Joe in
it from head to heels.   Then he fastened it at
the lad's throat with a long steel pin that had a
handle like a dagger.

"Why, I look just like a girl," said Joe,
glancing down at his feet.

"Very well, Miss Josephine," laughed Mr.
Deometari; "just take my arm."

The provost-marshal's office was on the op-
posite side of the public square from the tavern,
and Mr. Deometari, instead of following the
sidewalk, went through the court-house yard.
There was not much formality observed around
the office.   There was no sentinel stationed at
the door, which was opened (in response to
Mr. Deometari's knock) by a small negro boy.
Down a little passage-way, or hall, Mr. Deometari went, followed by Joe.   A light shone
from a door at the end of a passage on the left,
and into this door Mr. Deometari went without
ceremony.   There was not much furniture in
the room—four chairs, a lounge, and a table.   A
sword hung on the wall, between lithograph

portraits of General Lee and Stonewall Jackson; and on one side was a long array of pigeon-holes full of papers. A man sat at the table, and he was so busily engaged in writing that he nodded without looking up from his work.

The door attendant

"Henderson," said Mr. Deometari, "I have company to-night. I want you to know this young man. His name is Joe Maxwell. He is an honorary member of the Relief Committee."

At this Henderson wiped his pen on his head and laid it down. Then he peered across the table at Joe. The two candles that gave him light were so close to his eyes that they blinded him when he lifted his face.

"Maxwell, did you say?—All right, Mr. Maxwell; I am glad to see you. Excuse my hand; it is full of ink."

Mr. Henderson had a soft, gentle voice, and his hand, although it was splashed with ink, was as delicate as that of a woman.

"Is this the Mr. Henderson you were telling me about some time ago?" asked Joe, turning to Mr. Deometari. "I mean the Mr. Henderson who was sick when you retreated from Laurel Hill?"

"The same," said Mr. Deometari.

Mr. Henderson laughed softly to hide his surprise, pushed his chair back, and rose from his seat. Whatever he was going to say was left unsaid. At that moment a knock that echoed down the hallway came on the outer door, and it was followed almost immediately by the firm and measured tread of some newcomer. Then there appeared in the doorway the serene face of Mr. Archie Blandford. He glanced around the room half-smiling until his eyes fell on Joe, and then the shadowy smile gave place to an unmistakable frown. Joe saw it, and for the first time felt that his position was a peculiar one, to say the least. He began to feel very uncomfortable, and this feeling was not relieved by the curt nod of recognition that Mr. Blandford gave him. He was a sensitive lad, and it was not pleasant to realize that he was regarded as an intruder. He looked at Mr. Deometari, but that gentleman seemed to be absorbed in a study of the portraits on the wall. Mr. Blandford advanced a few steps into the room, hesitated, and then said, abruptly:

"Deo! let me see you a moment."

The two men went into the hall and as far as the outer door, and, although they talked in subdued tones, the passage took the place of a speaking-tube, and every word they uttered could be heard by Joe Maxwell and Mr. Henderson.

"Deo," said Mr. Blandford, "what under the sun is Maxwell doing here? He ought to be at home in bed."

"He is here," Mr. Deometari explained, "at my invitation."

"But your reason must tell you, Deo, that that child ought not to be mixed up in this night's business. It is almost certain to be serious."

"That is precisely the reason he is here," said Mr. Deometari. "I might preach to you from now until doomsday, and you'd never listen to me. But, with that boy looking at you, you'll keep your temper. I know you better than you know yourself. You came here to-night with your mind made up to do something rash. I read it in your face last night; I saw it in your eyes this morning; I hear it in your voice now. My dear fellow, it will never do in the world. You would ruin everything. What you intended to do, you won't dare to do with that boy looking at you. And there's another reason: if this man Johnson is to be taken out of the county, the best route is by Armour's Ferry, and Maxwell knows every foot of the road."

Then there was a pause, and Mr. Henderson went to the door and said:

"You two might as well come in here and have it out. We can hear every word you say."

They came back into the room, Mr. Blandford smiling, and Mr. Deometari a little flushed.

" I forgot to shake hands with you just now," said Mr. Blandford, going over to Joe and seizing the lad's hand.   " It wasn't because I don't like you."

" Thank you," replied Joe.   " I don't understand what you and Mr. Deo were talking about, but I don't wan't to be in the way."

" You are not in the way at all," said Mr. Deometari, emphatically.

" I should say not," exclaimed Mr. Blandford, heartily.   " Deo is right and I was wrong.   I'd be happy if I wasn't in anybody's way any more than you are.   You'll find out when you grow bigger that a man never gets too old to be a fool."   With that he reached under his overcoat and unbuckled a heavy pistol, and placed it on the mantel.—" You see," he said to Mr. Deometari, " I am making a complete surrender. I don't want to have that gun where I can get my hands on it when I see our friend Captain Johnson."

" You may buckle on your pistol," remarked Mr. Henderson, softly.   " You won't see the captain to-night."

"Thunderation!" exclaimed Mr. Deometari, springing to his feet. "We must see him! Pruitt is in the guard-house. Sick or well, Captain Johnson must travel with us this night. I don't want him killed or hurt, but the scoundrel shall strut around this town no more."

"It's just as I tell you," said Henderson, in his gentle way; "you'll not see him to-night."

Mr. Blandford laughed, as though he regarded the matter as a joke, while Mr. Henderson began to fumble among some papers on the table. He selected from these three little documents, which he spread out before him, one on the other. Then he looked at the other two men and smiled.

"Tom," said Mr. Deometari, "this is a very serious matter. You know this man Johnson as well as we do, and you know that the time has come to get rid of him."

"I know him a great deal better than either of you," said Mr. Henderson, still smiling, "and that is the reason he's not here to-night. That is the reason you won't see him."

Mr. Deometari paced back and forth on the floor, pulling his whiskers, while Mr. Blandford drummed impatiently on the table.

"The trouble is," Mr. Henderson went on, still addressing Mr. Deometari, "that we are both afraid of Archie Blandford's temper."

"Now, just listen at that!" exclaimed Mr. Blandford. "Why, you'll make this chap here think I'm vicious. He'll believe I'm a man-eater."

"We both know how he feels toward Captain Johnson," Mr. Henderson continued, not heeding the interruption, "and we have both been trying to prevent him from doing anything he might regret. I think your plan would have succeeded; and I'm glad you brought Maxwell, anyhow, because I like to meet a bright boy once in a while; but my plan is the best, after all, for Captain Johnson is gone."

Mr. Deometari stopped walking the floor, and sat down. "Tell us about it."

"Well," said Mr. Henderson, "here is some correspondence that came to Captain Johnson through the post-office. There are three letters. We will call this number one:

"'Sir: It has been noticed that you have refused to forward supplies intended for the wives and children of Confederate soldiers.

This refers especially to the wife and children of one John Pruitt.'

" There is no signature," said Mr. Henderson. " This "—taking up another document— " we will call number two."

" ' Sir : It is known that no supplies have left this post for the wife and children of one John Pruitt. Will the Relief Committee have to act ?

" Here," continued Mr. Henderson, " is the last. It is number three :

" ' Sir : John Pruitt is in jail, where he can not help himself. The Relief Committee will meet to-morrow night. Hold yourself in readiness to hear again the story of the retreat from Laurel Hill.' "

" Well ? " said Mr. Deometari, as Mr. Henderson paused.

" Well, the man was worried nearly to death. He was in a continual fidget. At last he came to me and talked the matter over. That was yesterday. We went over the Laurel Hill incidents together, and I used Archie Blandford's name pretty freely. The upshot of it was that I advised Captain Johnson to report to the commander of the post in Macon, and he took my advice."

"Do I look like a dangerous man?" asked Mr. Blandford, turning to Joe.

"Not now," replied Joe. "But your eyes are very bright."

"I wish to goodness they were as bright as yours!" said Mr. Blandford, laughing.

"So we've had all our trouble for nothing," Mr. Deometari suggested.

"Oh, no," said Mr. Henderson; "we've been saved a great deal of trouble. Johnson is gone, and I have here an order for Pruitt's release."

"If we had known all this," remarked Mr. Deometari, "Maxwell would be safe in bed, where I suspect he ought to be.—My son," he went on, "it is a pity to have you riding back and forth in the night."

"Just to please a fat man with the whimsies," Mr. Blandford observed.

"Oh, it is no trouble to me," Joe protested. "It is almost like a book, only I don't exactly understand it all. What were you going to do with Captain Johnson?"

"Me? oh, I—well, the fact is, Deo was commanding my regiment to-night," replied Mr. Blandford. He seemed to be embarrassed.

"It is all very simple," said Mr. Deometari.

" When you get a little older you'll find a great many people like Captain Johnson. He had a little power, and he has used it so as to turn all the people here against him. Another trouble is, that he used to belong to the regulars, where the discipline is as strict as it can be. He has tried to be too strict here, and these Confederate people won't stand it. The private soldier thinks he is as good as a commissioned officer, and sometimes better. A provost-marshal is a sort of military chief of police, and, when his commander is as far away as Macon, he can do a good deal of harm, especially if he has a streak of meanness running through him. Johnson has made enemies here by the hundred. Worst of all, he has treated the wives of soldiers very badly. You know all about his spite at John Pruitt. We were going to take him to-night to Armour's Ferry, put him across the river, and give him to understand that we could get along without him."

"And he would never come back?" asked Joe.

"No," said Mr. Deometari, "he would never come back."

"Was Mr. Blandford very mad with him?" inquired the lad.

"Yes, I was," that gentleman admitted, laughing a little and looking uncomfortable. "He had me arrested once, and tried to make me shovel sand into a barrel that was open at both ends. What do you think of that?"

"I think it must have been very funny," said Joe, laughing heartily.

"I reckon it was funny," observed Mr. Blandford, grimly, "but the rascal wouldn't have enjoyed the fun if it hadn't been for this big fat man here."

"You are not referring to me, I hope," said Mr. Henderson, so seriously that the rest burst out laughing.

"Come, now," Mr. Deometari suggested. "Let's let in some fresh air on poor John Pruitt."

There was nothing more to be done after Mr. Pruitt was released from the guard-house, and so Joe mounted his horse and cantered off to the plantation. Butterfly was very glad to have his head turned in that direction, and he went so swiftly that in the course of an hour Joe was at home and in bed. His mind was so full of what he had seen and heard that he went over it all in his slumber. Mr. Deometari, chunky as he was, took the place of Porthos, the big musketeer; Mr. Blandford was D'Artagnan; Mr. Henderson was the sleek and slender one (Aramis) whose name Joe could not remember in his dreams; and even Mr. Pruitt grew into a romantic figure.

CHAPTER XIV.

THE CURTAIN FALLS.

SOMEHOW, after Joe Maxwell's experience with Mr. Deometari, Mr. Blandford, and the rest, events of importance seemed to follow each other more rapidly. Some of them were surprising, and all confusing. It was in the month of July that Atlanta was taken by General Sherman. A few weeks afterward, Harbert, while cleaning and oiling the old Washington No. 2 hand-press in *The Countryman* office, told Joe that the Federal army would come marching through the county before long.

"Who told you?" asked Joe.

"De word done come," replied Harbert "Hit bleeze ter be so, kaze all de niggers done hear talk un it. We-all will wake up some er deze odd-come-shorts an' fin' de Yankees des a-swarmin' all 'roun' here."

"What are you going to do?" Joe inquired, laughing.

"Oh, you kin laugh, Marse Joe, but deyer comin'. What I gwine do? Well, suh, I'm gwine ter git up an' look at um, an' may be tip my hat ter some er de big-bugs 'mongst um, an' den I'm gwine on 'bout my business. I don't speck deyer gwine ter bodder folks what don't bodder dem, is dey?"

Joe had forgotten this conversation until it was recalled to his mind one morning shortly after his night ride to Hillsborough. General Sherman had swung loose from Atlanta, and was marching down through middle Georgia. The people that Joe saw went about with anxious faces, and even the negroes were frightened. Before this vast host all sorts of rumors fled, carrying fear and consternation to the peaceful plantations. At last, one cold, drizzly day in November, Joe Maxwell, trudging along the road on his way to the printing-office, heard the clatter of hoofs behind him, and two horsemen in blue came galloping along. They reined up their horses, and inquired the distance to Hillsborough, and then went galloping on again. They were couriers carrying dispatches from the Twentieth Army Corps to General Sherman.

There was hurrying to and fro on the plantation after this. The horses and mules were driven to a remote field in which there was a large swamp. Joe carried Butterfly and teth-

Even the negroes were frightened.

ered him in the very middle of the swamp, where he could get plenty of water to drink and young cane to eat. During the next ten hours the plantation, just as Harbert predicted, fairly swarmed with foraging parties of Federals. Guided by some of the negroes, they found the horses and mules and other stock and drove them off, and, when Joe heard of it, he felt like crying over the loss of Butterfly. The horse did not belong to him, but he had trained it from a colt, and it was his whenever he wanted to use it, day or night. Yet Butterfly was soon forgotten in the excitement and confusion created by the foragers, who swept through the plantations, levying in the name of war on the live-stock, and ransacking the not too well-filled smoke-houses and barns in search of supplies.

Joe Maxwell saw a good deal of these foragers, and he found them all, with one exception, to be good-humored. The exception was a German, who could scarcely speak English enough to make himself understood. This German, when he came to the store-room where the hats were kept, wanted to take off as many as his horse could carry, and he became very angry when Joe protested. He grew so angry, in fact, that he would have fired the building. He lit a match, drew together a lot of old papers and other rubbish, and was in the act of firing

it, when an officer ran in and gave him a tremendous paddling with the flat of his sword.
It was an exhibition as funny as a scene in the
circus, and Joe enjoyed it as thoroughly as he
could under the circumstances. By night, all
the foragers had disappeared.

The army had gone into camp at Denham's
Mill, and Joe supposed that it would march on to
Hillsborough, but in this he was mistaken. It
turned sharply to the left the next morning and
marched toward Milledgeville. Joe had aim-
lessly wandered along this road, as he had done
a hundred times before, and finally seated himself on the fence near an old school-house, and
began to whittle on a rail. Before he knew it
the troops were upon him. He kept his seat,
and the Twentieth Army Corps, commanded by
General Slocum, passed in review before him.
It was an imposing array as to numbers, but not
as to appearance. For once and for all, so far
as Joe was concerned, the glamour and romance
of war were dispelled. The skies were heavy
with clouds, and a fine, irritating mist sifted
down. The road was more than ankle-deep in
mud, and even the fields were boggy. There
was nothing gay about this vast procession,

with its tramping soldiers, its clattering horsemen, and its lumbering wagons, except the temper of the men.   They splashed through the
mud, cracking their jokes and singing snatches
of songs.

A forager.

Joe Maxwell, sitting on the fence, was the
subject of many a jest, as the good-humored
men marched by.

"Hello, Johnny!   Where's your parasol?"

"Jump down, Johnny, and let me kiss you good-by!"

"Johnny, if you are tired, get up behind and ride!"

"Run and get your trunk, Johnny, and get aboard!"

"He's a bushwhacker, boys. If he bats his eyes, I'm a-goin' to dodge!"

"Where's the rest of your regiment, Johnny?"

"If there was another one of 'em a-settin' on the fence, on t'other side, I'd say we was surrounded!"

These and hundreds of other comments, exclamations, and questions, Joe was made the target of; and, if he stood the fire of them with unusual calmness, it was because this huge panorama seemed to him to be the outcome of some wild dream. That the Federal army should be plunging through that peaceful region, after all he had seen in the newspapers about Confederate victories, seemed to him to be an impossibility. The voices of the men, and their laughter, sounded vague and insubstantial. It was surely a dream that had stripped war of its glittering trappings and its flying banners. It was

surely the distortion of a dream that tacked on
to this procession of armed men droves of cows,
horses, and mules, and wagon-loads of bateaux!
Joe had read of pontoon bridges, but he had
never heard of a pontoon train, nor did he know
that bateaux were a part of the baggage of this
invading army.

But it all passed after a while, and then Joe
discovered that he had not been dreaming at
all. He jumped from the fence and made his
way home through the fields. Never before,
since its settlement, had such peace and quiet
reigned on the plantation. The horses and
mules were gone, and many of the negro cabins
were empty. Harbert was going about as busy
as ever, and some of the older negroes were in
their accustomed places, but the younger ones,
especially those who, by reason of their field-
work, had not been on familiar terms with their
master and mistress, had followed the Federal
army. Those that remained had been informed
by the editor that they were free; and so it happened, in the twinkling of an eye, that the old
things had passed away and all was new.

In a corner of the fence, not far from the
road, Joe found an old negro woman shivering

and moaning. Near her lay an old negro man, his shoulders covered with an old ragged shawl.

" Who is that lying there ? " asked Joe.

" It my ole man, suh."

" What is the matter with him ? "

" He dead, suh! But, bless God, he died free ! " *

It was a pitiful sight, and a pitiable ending of the old couple's dream of freedom. Harbert and the other negroes buried the old man, and the old woman was made comfortable in one of the empty cabins; she never ceased to bless " little marster," as she called Joe, giving him all the credit for everything that was done for her. Old as she was, she and her husband had followed the army for many a weary mile on the road to freedom. The old man found it in the fence corner, and a few weeks later the old woman found it in the humble cabin.

The next morning, as Joe Maxwell was loitering around the printing-office, talking to the editor, Butterfly came galloping up, ridden by Mink, who was no longer a runaway.

---

* This incident has had many adaptations. It occurred just as it is given here, and was published afterward in *The Countryman*.

" I seed you put 'im out in de swamp dar, Mars' Joe, an' den I seed some er de yuther niggers gwine dar 'long wid dem Yankee mens, an' I say ter myse'f dat I better go dar an' git 'im; so I tuck 'im down on de river, an' here he is.   He mayn't be ez fat ez he wuz, but he des ez game ez he yever is been."

Joe was pleased, and the editor was pleased; and it happened that Mink became one of the tenants on the plantation, and after a while he bought a little farm of his own, and prospered and thrived.

But this is carrying a simple chronicle too far.   It can not be spun out here and now so as to show the great changes that have been wrought—the healing of the wounds of war; the lifting up of a section from ruin and poverty to prosperity; the molding of the beauty, the courage, the energy, and the strength of the old civilization into the new; the gradual uplifting of a lowly race.   All these things can not be told of here.   The fire burns low, and the tale is ended.

The plantation newspaper was issued a little while longer, but in a land filled with desolation and despair its editor could not hope to see it survive. A larger world beckoned to Joe Maxwell, and he went out into it. And it came about that on every side he found loving hearts to comfort him and strong and friendly hands to guide him. He found new associations and formed new ties. In a humble way he made a name for himself, but the old plantation days still live in his dreams.

THE END.